Playing For You

A Wearside Story Prequel

Ellie White

ISBN: 978-1-7396174-4-8

Imprint: E White Publishing

Editing: Aimee Walker

Cover Design: Ellie White - Image Copyright Purchased from Canva.

Also by Ellie White

Standalone Novels

Love & London

Love in the Wings

A Wearside Story

Book 0.5 - Playing For You (A Wearside Story Novella)

Book 1 - Playing For Her

Book 2 - Playing For Real - April 2024

A Romance Duet - Novellas

A Romance For Christmas - December 2023

The Romance Retreat - July 2024

Playing For You

For all my sporty girlies...

No matter the sport you play, I hope you see yourself

within these pages.

Playing For You

CHAPTER ONE

Natasha

For the fourth time in sixty-seven minutes, the opposing team's star striker goes on the attack. She keeps the ball close as she weaves her way through my defensive line and mere seconds later, when her boot connects sharply with the ball, she fires it straight towards the bottom-right corner of my goal.

Without a second thought for my own well-being, I dive to the ground with my arms outstretched in an attempt to claw back some dignity in this match. The ball barely grazes my fingertips as it hurtles past me, hitting the back of the net with that all-too-familiar swoosh, leaving me red faced and covered in mud and grass from the drizzle drenched pitch.

"Fuck!" Rolling over to my front and up onto my knees, I pound my fists hard into the grass like a toddler having a tantrum. I curse and yell and scream into the mud, slapping my gloved hands hard to the ground to push myself to my feet with a growl.

Our opposition are understandably elated, celebrating loudly as their fans cheer in unison.

On our side of the stadium, our fans are eerily silent as the rainfall mirrors the atmosphere. Many fans have left already, leaving vast empty spaces in the stands, and I don't blame them, this is the latest in a long line of losses for Wearside Women.

"Pull it together and communicate, come on!" our team captain, Brooke, shouts across the pitch to our defence. "Keep it tight and close the gaps! We're better than this, girls!"

This is embarrassing, the voice in my head screams. *Pathetic.*

Useless. Talentless—

"Ha'way, Lasses!" I clap my hands loudly and try my best to keep some of that team spirit our coach always bangs on about.

Fake it 'til you make it, that's what they say, right?

Your parents are right. The statement in my head jolts me. *Failure, failure, failure.*

The cold rain falls in larger droplets now, splashing on my face. My breaths come fast and harsh, leaving little puffs of steam suspended in the air.

I can't do this.

A whistle from the ref signals for play to continue, but I can't bring myself to take the goal kick. Instead, I stand with the ball in my hands, resolve weakening as all the fight evaporates from my body, leaving only nausea and disappointment in its place.

"Come on!" one of the opposition team shouts at me. "Stop wasting time!" another adds.

I look at them all watching me expectantly, and then to

the ball that I let drop to the floor. Confusion ripples across the pitch from both sides.

Raising my arm, I signal to the dugout that I need to come off, and a moment later, my feet carry me from the pitch and into the dressing room showers where I sit under the stream of warm water, fully clothed with my head in my hands for the remainder of the match.

Brooke Davison is my best friend. She also happens to be my captain and teammate, and this means she usually bears the brunt of my bad attitude. Today is no different as we sit side by side on the wooden slats of the bench in the dressing room. Our eyes are closed, but only her breathing is even and steady as we 'meditate'.

"Natasha," she says in her calm and soothing voice that I equal parts love and hate, "breathe with me. You sound like the Big Bad Wolf huffing and puffing and blowing football stadiums down."

"This isn't working," I respond through gritted teeth.

I open one eye and sneak a peek at her. Her pretty face is soft and relaxed, unlike the frown distorting my features.

"Close your eyes please, Natasha," she says, her tone nice and calm.

"How do you do that?"

She didn't even open her eyes to look at me. "I can feel you glaring at me."

I silently mock her, mouthing her words sarcastically. "I can feel that too."

"Fine." I close my eyes and shake out my arms. "I'm ready, let's do this."

"Okay, listen to my breathing and match my rhythm." I do as she says, breathing in and out in a slow rhythm and gradually, my muscles do begin to relax, which is annoying because I didn't want her to be right. "Let go of the past. You can't change it, but we can learn from it."

"Okay, Raffki!" I snort and she flicks my thigh. "Ow. I'm sorry, but this is stupid."

"Then you need to find a way that works for you, because whatever this is"—she gestures in my general direction—"isn't healthy."

"I'm too old to change now, too long in the tooth."

"You're twenty-six!" she says in disbelief. "Natasha, I'm serious. I'm not going to address what happened with you out there just yet, I'll give you a few days to gather your thoughts first, but I need you to know I'm worried about you."

"Honestly, I'm done," I lie, and she knows it.

"Today isn't all on you. We had a bad game, we all made mistakes, and this is our time to reflect on that so we can move forward."

"Davison, you're up," Physio Phillipa comes to my rescue when she calls across the room, letting Brooke know it's her turn for cold water therapy.

She pats my shoulder before she heads off to the ice bath and I sulk for a little while on my own. I try to breathe like Brooke taught me, but just as I feel my muscles relaxing again, the intrusive thoughts return.

CHAPTER TWO

Luke

"I've organised the plants together to make it easier for you," my sister Hannah says the second I walk through the door to her open-plan riverside apartment. Natural light floods through the French windows leading to the balcony. "Hey, Luke, lovely to see you. How are you doing?... Oh, I'm fantastic, thanks so much for asking... You look great, bro... Thanks, sis, I had my hair and beard trimmed this morning like you told me to because you said I was starting to look like Bigfoot," I converse with myself sarcastically, but she pays no notice.

"Mmm-hmm, great. These plants here need watering once a week and spritzing with the spray in the morning and afternoon." She points to a number of potted plants crammed onto the kitchen windowsill and fixes me with a stern look, checking I'm listening. "Rotate them daily so they grow evenly."

"Got it."

"I've organised their food," she continues.

"Food? They're plants."

"Plants need food. Orchid food, rose food and everything else food," she instructs, pointing to the bottles lined up on her cluttered bookshelf. "Don't worry, I've left you a binder with instructions."

"Wonderful. Now, don't you have a plane to catch?" I clap my hands twice in encouragement.

"Don't forget Stanley, he's on the balcony," she adds as she pulls on her coat and rucksack.

"You've named them?"

"Yes, they all have names. They're written on the little lolly sticks in the soil." Of course, they all have names. "Okay. I'm ready," she adds with a squeal of delight.

I haul my sister's backpack down to my car and place it in the boot. She's heading to Australia for three months to conduct research into her master's in sports psychology and is leaving me in charge of her flat and her *babies,* aka her plants.

Her trip couldn't have come at a better time for me. I sold my house to move into a bigger one, which isn't quite ready yet, and by that, I mean it's still a building site. So, instead of paying for a hotel for three months, I'm moving into her flat in Sunderland city centre. It's a win win for both of us.

It's mid-morning when I drive her to the airport. Luckily the traffic isn't too heavy and we make it to the airport with plenty time. We head straight for check-in and then Starbucks for one last coffee together.

"You're going to be okay, right?" she asks as she pours sugar into her cup and stirs, her eyebrows knitting together.

13

"You're the one going off to another country, I'll be in the exact same spot you left me in when you get back."

"That's my worry!"

I'm a gamer. I program and design games specifically for PlayStation and Xbox. It's intense work, especially when designing the initial concepts and coding. Therefore, I've developed a habit of dropping off the face of the earth for days at a time until my baby sister drags me back to the land of the living.

"I'm a twenty-eight-year-old man, I'll be fine."

"Well, I've set alarms on Alexa to give you reminders anyway."

The next ten minutes pass in companionable silence as we people-watch and drink our coffees until it's time to walk Hannah to security.

"Don't forget to send me updates on the game," she says as we come to a stop outside the security entrance. She turns to face me which makes what I'm about to tell her way harder.

"About the game…I've decided to withdraw my funding application."

At first, she doesn't say anything, she just stares at me, completely disgust on her face.

Quickly recovering, she lets me have it.

"No. You. Are. Not. Luke Ramshaw, pull yourself together for fuck's sake," she says, sounding just like Mam. Mam would have never sworn at me though.

"I don't know how I'll get it done, Han. I'm running out of time."

"This is a huge opportunity for you and your business. You can't throw that away. What you need is a little motivation. If you speak to the club, you know Auntie Mel will help you."

It's a good idea, one that's crossed my mind already, if only I could bring myself to make the call. "I'll think about it, but for now you need to get going. Message me on your stopovers, let me know you're safe," I say, changing the subject, tugging her close to me for a hug when we reach airport security. "And promise you'll ring me when you get to Sydney. I don't care what time it is."

She hugs me back tightly, letting the previous subject go.

"I promise I'll call you when I can, but, Luke, I'm a big girl, you don't need to be so overprotective. You should be making the most of not having me around to cramp your style. Better still, get back on the dating apps and have a good time!"

I hit her with an unamused glare. Overprotective is all I know. Dad died suddenly from a brain aneurysm when I was two and Hannah was a newborn. Then we lost Mam when I was eighteen, so I took custody of her, taking on the role of parent and big brother. Since then, it's been the two of us and this will be the longest we've ever been apart.

"I'm just saying, it's been a while since you've dated."

I don't tell her that the reason I haven't dated for a few years is because, as more than one ex put it, I'm too 'overprotective' and 'over- bearing'. It'll give her more fuel to add to the fire.

Instead, I say, "Yeah okay, I'll think about it." To get her off my back.

She stands on her tiptoes to ruffle my hair and punches my arm, her way of saying she'll miss me, I'm sure.

"Bye, Luke! See you in three months!" she calls out with one Final free-spirited wave.

I wave back and watch her until she's out of sight, blending in with other excited travellers. Hannah's a grown woman, she's tough, smart, and sensible.

She's going to be fine. I'm going to be fine.

Oh god, who am I trying to kid? I'm already an anxious wreck.

Back at her flat, I take the time to find a home for my gaming equipment in her living room, avoiding the surfaces where the plants reside. I brought everything I need for three months of work: four monitors, various speakers and a PC I built from scratch when I was at uni.

On the coffee table, I neatly line up various controllers and connect my PlayStation and Xbox to the big TV on her wall. Before long, the space is organised and looks like something you'd expect to see on the Starship Enterprise, flashing lights and sleek black and silver electronics everywhere. I survey the set-up with wonder and adoration as if I'm looking at my first-born child.

I know I'm procrastinating when I make myself another coffee using Hannah's fancy machine and sit on the balcony overlooking the River Wear. I need to make that call and as I toy with my phone, I can't put it off any longer.

Raising the phone to my ear, I listen to the ringing until a familiar comforting voice answers that hurtles me ten years in the past.

I swallow down the lump in my throat and speak. "Hey, Auntie Mel. It's Luke."

CHAPTER THREE

Natasha

Unlike the weekend, Wednesday's match isn't as bad a loss. I only let one goal past me this time, and I manage to last the whole ninety minutes without having a complete breakdown.

"Seriously, I'm about to lose my fucking shit!" I say for the umpteenth time tonight. Okay, I might not have had a breakdown today, but I'm so fucking close to it tonight. This time it's not football related or even a problem I've brought on myself.

My lovely, sweet and silent next-door neighbour has gone away for three months.

My lovely, sweet and silent next-door neighbour's inconsiderate, video-game-playing brother is !at-sitting. Night after night, I've had to endure the sounds of guns shooting and stupid zombies groaning and moaning through the wall that connects our living rooms.

"I just want to fucking sleep," I whine.

"Surely it's not so bad from your bedroom," Bridget reasons, although she has to raise her voice to be heard which completely invalidates her point. Bridget O'Leary is my oldest

18

friend. We met at primary school after her family moved from Ireland, and now she's head of the Wearside FC PR department. It's literally in her nature to be rational and non-confrontational at all times.

"Oh, you can. That godawful sound travels! Four nights this has gone on for! He's a fucking insomniac or something," I shout back, again struggling to be heard at my normal level.

"Why don't you go and politely ask him to turn the volume down? He probably doesn't realise you can hear it," Brooke suggests, also trying to be helpful. Only thing is, I don't want helpful resolutions. I want my closest friends to share in my complete and utter rage. She winces as a particularly brutal sound travels through the wall at this point I'm beginning to feel sorry for the zombies.

"Fuck it, let's go!" I stand abruptly from my sofa.

Dressed in our pyjamas and slippers, despite their protests, I drag both girls into the hallway with me for support. Bridget and Brooke share an apartment a few floors above me, so it's not strange to find us wandering the corridors between each other's flats in PJs. I can't say I've ever stormed the hallways of the building waging war though, so this is new for us.

When I come to a halt outside his door, I knock a little harder than I intend to. No one answers, so I try again harder. He's in there; his game is still playing the sounds of slaughtered zombies!

I look back to the girls who are watching me, clearly worried I'm on the verge of some homicidal meltdown.

19

"Maybe we should come back in the morning when you've calmed down?" Bridget whispers, leaning forward slightly to where I stand ahead of them.

"No fucking way! I'll bet any money he's a deadbeat gamer who doesn't work and thinks it's perfectly fine to play video games all night and sleep all day with no care or consideration for those of us who actually contribute to society."

"Do you not think you're being a little judgemental when you don't know the guy?" Brooke asks.

Yes, I'm being judgemental, but I'm pissed off, so whatever.

Turning back to the door, I ignore her and do what any other batshit person would do in this situation and bang on the door, loud, hard and fast, until he answers, half-naked, looking a little panicked.

"Shit, what's going on?" he asks, looking between the three of us, confusion etched in his beautiful face. Fuck, I was not expecting this! "Are you okay?" He glances down the corridor for signs of danger that don't exist.

I know it's stereotypical of me and since I'm a female footballer who hears all the stereotypes, I should know better, but when you see gamers in movies and on TV, they're always super nerdy; pale and thin from staying indoors all day, but this guy... Shit, he's gorgeous.

He's tall. Very tall. I'm above average height for a woman at five foot eight and this guy has an easy six inches on me. He's toned without being overly ripped. His shirtless torso is tight and firm with a light sprinkling of dark chest hair, and he has the most beautiful collarbones I've ever seen. I didn't even realise I had a thing for collarbones, but hey, it's apparently my new kink because I want to lick them.

But it's his eyes that really suck me in. They're the most brilliant shade of forest green I've ever seen. And they're staring right at me.

Shit, *he's* staring right at me, waiting for me to speak. His lips quirk as he notices and my gaze follows the curves.

"You're loud!" I snap myself out of the trance he's pulled me into. "I'm sorry?" His eyebrows pucker ever so slightly at my aggression.

"Your games are loud," I say, steadying my voice and recovering from my initial shock. I plant my hands firmly on my hips, taking a step closer to him.

I'm obviously not very intimidating because he smirks at me, actually fucking smirks, and leans against the doorframe, crossing his arms over his chest. Holy forearms, he has those too, all lean muscle and thick veins and…I'm losing focus again.

"I wear a headset," he says simply, no apology in sight.

"Your headset is obviously not working," I reply through gritted teeth.

"I'm sorry, I'll check out the speakers because you shouldn't be able to hear a thing." He's cool and collected when he runs his hand through his tousled deep brown hair.

"Well, make sure you do because some of us actually have jobs to go to and need a decent night sleep," I say snidely.

"Come on, let's go," I add for the benefit of the girls behind me who have been useless this entire time.

"You know, when you introduce yourself to someone, you're supposed to give them your name," he says as I walk away, a cocky confidence oozing out of him.

"And why is that?" I ask, turning back to face him, ignoring the giggles from Brooke and Bridget.

"It's good manners." He smirks at me once more from his doorway. "I'm Luke."

"I'm Bridget, this is Brooke, and the grumpy one is Natasha," Bridget says, helpfully looking between us when I don't respond.

"Sort the noise out so I can sleep and we won't have any other issues!" I grunt, throwing my hands in the air and storming back into my apartment.

"Goodnight, Natasha," he calls after me, and honestly, I don't hate the way that sounds.

CHAPTER FOUR

Natasha

Obediently, I follow Mam through the hallway of my childhood home to the dining room. It's hard to miss the large portrait held in a gilded frame. It's a photo of me standing between my proud parents at my university graduation or as Dad refers to it: a constant reminder of how much of a disappointment I am.

My parents are both solicitors at our family firm, Borthwick Law. My granddad, the original Borthwick, started the business and my dad started working there right out of secondary school. Throughout my life, it was well known that his intention was for me to follow in his footsteps, but all my five years studying law did was confirm that I absolutely did not want to work in that field.

I'm not cut out for an office.

"Hi, Dad," I say, walking into the dining room where he sits at the head of the table, reading a broadsheet newspaper.

"Darling." He offers me his cheek without looking up.

"How are you?" I press a kiss to his ageing skin before taking a seat at the formal place setting to his right. Dad is always impeccably smart, clean shaven and wears a freshly ironed shirt and trousers no matter where he is or what his plans are.

"Oh, you know, just another day of not having an heir to the firm," he says as if he's joking, but it's been said enough times that I know he's serious. This time I doubt it took him two minutes to get his jibe in. "I saw the result the other night, it was on the news. They were talking about you." My heart sinks to my toes. I learned a long time ago not to read articles about myself and to fast forward through the highlights when they cover Wearside Women. My dad, on the other hand, has not.

"Oh right… We're going through a rough patch as a team at the moment but with a little hard work, I'm sure we'll pick it up again."

"Do you not think it's about time you give up the hobby and do something meaningful with your life?" he asks, placing the paper down in front of him. "You could be out there making a difference to people's lives."

Here we go.

"I love my job, Dad." Even I can tell I sound less than convincing.

"Sweetheart, the best thing happened at work this week," Mam says, saving me from the conversation as she places our plates in front of us.

"Yeah?" I ask, feigning enthusiasm. If Dad tries to shame me into joining the family business, Mam tries to convince me that working in law is the best thing in the world. She amps up her job satisfaction at every opportunity to try and get me to see the error of my ways.

"A woman came in with her son who's setting up a new business and needed some advice. It's so satisfying when you get to help people, you know. The look on his face made all that challenging work worth it." She clutches the napkin she's carrying to her heart.

"Sounds great, Mam."

"It really was."

She disappears into the kitchen again, returning a moment later with her own plate and takes a seat opposite me on Dad's other side.

In general, my mood is lower than it has been for weeks, but I don't think they notice as we eat in our usual silence. When we finish, I excuse myself for a breather by offering to clear the plates and stack the dishwasher.

"Dad isn't getting any younger," Mam says when I return to the table a few minutes later. She glances across at Dad who has gone back to his paper, completely uninterested in my company. "And neither am I," she adds.

"Are you trying to tell me one of you is sick?" Panic surges through me. Is that what tonight is about?

"No, of course not. I'm just saying, we'd like to retire soon, and the firm will be your responsibility. You'll need to go back to school for a refresher before you take over, of course. It has been a few years since you graduated."

"I'm not a lawyer, Mam. I don't want to take over."

"This is our family legacy, Natasha," Dad says sternly,

slamming his paper down on the table, making me jump. "You're our only child. It's up to you to keep it going when we're gone."

"But I don't want to, Dad. I'm sorry."

"Do you realise how juvenile you sound? You have five, maybe ten years of your footballing career left at the very most. Then what?"

"I don't know. I have plenty of time to decide what path I take when I'm done playing."

"That's the best part. You don't have to decide because you have the law firm, sweetheart," Mam adds calmly with a sickly sweet smile.

"I don't want it." Short of stomping my feet, I have no idea how to get this across to them. "I don't want the firm!"

"Why do you have to be such an ungrateful little girl? After everything we've done for you. This is your legacy."

"I'm not ungrateful! And I'm not a little girl! I want to live my life how I see fit." I stand abruptly, refusing to take any more. It's the last straw. "I have to go. I've got a match tomorrow and I need a good night's sleep."

"We'll see you on the six o-clock news then," Dad snaps, and with that I walk out, slamming the door behind me like the child they think I am.

I'm used to these nights ending like this, but it doesn't make it hurt any less. Tears sting my eyes all the way home and when I eventually reach the door to my apartment, the one person I don't need to see is coming out of his.

"Natasha? Are you okay?" His voice is full of concern,

but I'm a fucking coward so I ignore him, closing myself away in the safety of my flat like I have every other time I've seen him since our run-in the other night.

As I lie in bed a little while later and everything is quiet, I realise I miss the sounds of Luke's video games. Because without the incessant shooting and zombie cries, the voices and doubts that play in my mind as I stare at my ceiling are much harder to ignore.

CHAPTER FIVE

Luke

"So, shall we talk about this proposal you have?" Auntie Mel asks as I sit across from her in her office at the Wearside FC training academy. She's trying her best to keep her poker face in place, but any minute now, the grin she's been suppressing since I walked through the door fifteen minutes ago is going to burst out of her.

Mel isn't a blood-related auntie; she was Mam's best friend. They both played professional football here at Wearside Women when I was a kid. The club became a second family to us when we lost Dad. We were here so often it was like we lived here.

Mam died here too. She walked out of the tunnel into a packed stadium and five minutes later suffered a heart attack and collapsed in the penalty box while Hannah and I watched from the stands with thousands of others.

After I lost Mam, I grew to despise the game that cruelly took her away from us, but I'd still bring Hannah here almost every day. My sister loves any kind of sport, but especially football and I couldn't take that away from her. I'd drop her off after school while I went to my uni classes on an evening. When she was old enough to drive, she didn't need me to bring her anymore, so I stopped coming altogether.

It was easier to leave this world behind than confront my feelings head on and unfortunately that meant leaving Mel behind too.

But the way she's welcomed me back with open arms, as if I didn't turn my back on her for all these years, makes me realise what a big mistake I made and now I'm here, I hope I get a chance to rectify that.

I clear my throat. "I've designed a basic concept for a game based on women's football. Like FIFA but for the Women's Super League to start, hopefully extending to the Championship. I need to pitch for the licence and apply for funding and I've hit a mental block. In return for sponsorship next season, I'd like access to the academy and the team to help with the development of the video game," I say. "I can't offer you exclusivity in the marketing, but I can guarantee Wearside Women will be heavily promoted within the game and the advertising campaigns."

"You don't need to offer sponsorship, Luke. You're welcome here anytime and we're happy to help." Her voice is kind and reassuring. She knows how hard it was for me to come here today.

"I've looked at the club records, Mel. Cash is low and if you get relegated this season, you'll lose your primary sponsor. You'll never get that level of sponsorship from another company if you go down a league. The team won't be able to survive it,

especially not when the men's first team are in the same position."
I meet her gaze, adding, "I can't let that happen to her club when she fought so hard to get the women's team off the ground in the first place."

She nods her silent understanding. "I'm impressed. You did your homework. I do need to sign new players if we're going to survive this season and there are a few in the academy I've had my eye on. If you're serious about this"—she produces a manilla file, handing it over her cluttered desk to me—"these are our current sponsorship packages."

I open the folder as she watches me intently. I already looked into their sponsorship packages whilst doing my research on the club, but I still peruse the page.

"I'll take full secondary sponsorship for three years until the game is released. Then we can negotiate again, if necessary." I close the folder and place it down gently.

"On behalf of the club welcome back to the family," Mel says with a grin, offering her hand and we shake on the deal. "Bridget O'Leary is our head of PR and marketing. I'll get her to come and see you to sort out the finer details, while I head out with the girls for this morning's training session. If you're happy to stick around, I can introduce you when they're done."

"That sounds great," I say excitedly, hope already starting to bubble up in my stomach. "Would you mind if we don't tell them who Mam was right away though? It's not that I don't want them to know, but people tend to look at me differently when they know."

"Of course," she agrees, then picks up the phone and asks Bridget to come fetch me.

Familiarity settles over me for a second, but I have trouble placing the name until a beautiful woman with jet black hair appears in the doorframe of Mel's office. Unlike the last time I saw Bridget—dressed in pyjamas with Natasha and their other friend Brooke in the hallway—she's a stone faced professional, her hair styled in neat Jessica Rabbit waves, dressed in a perfectly fitted burgundy dress and heels so high they look impossible to walk in.

"This is Luke Ramshaw. His company is going to be a secondary sponsor this season in exchange for the expertise of the club. Could you draw up the sponsorship contract please?" Mel says, and Bridget turns to face me, recognition dawning on her.

"This is wonderful!" Her eyes shine with excitement, although I can't work out why given the complicated situation I have with her friend who's obviously still mad at me. "What exactly do you mean 'expertise of the club'?"

"Access to the players, staff and the facilities. While you're at it, sort him a season card for the rest of the season and get him a temporary ID badge for the academy." Mel stands, gathering an iPad and notebook from her desk, so I follow suit. "I'll arrange to have a copy of our schedule for the next few weeks sent over to you this afternoon, so you can plan what you need around that. Bridget will accompany you in the meantime and we'll call a meeting in the media room to announce it to the team after the session."

"Thank you, Mel. I really appreciate it," I say sincerely before turning to Bridget who is still grinning like a Cheshire cat. "Lead the way."

An hour later, when all the official documents are signed and I've cleared the air with Bridget, we're standing in the media room waiting for the team to arrive.

"Nervous?" she asks as the door creaks open and players begin to file in.

"No," I lie. "A little."

She laughs. "Don't worry, once she gets over the shock it'll all be fine."

"She?" I ask, but she doesn't have time to respond before I turn and meet the shocked eyes of Natasha.

CHAPTER SIX

Natasha

A bolt of what can only be described as lightning strikes me, rooting me to the spot.

"Natasha, is something wrong?" Coach calls out as the traffic jam I'm causing on the stairs get restless.

Luke recovers from his surprise long before I do, his features relaxing into a soft smile as his familiar eyes warm to me. I hate to say this, but he looks fucking good. Maybe it's the shirt sleeves he's got rolled up to his elbows showing off those delicious forearms or the fact I know exactly what he's hiding under his smart-casual attire. Whatever it is, it's working for me big time.

"Natasha?" Coach asks again, and I realise I'm still staring at him. Christ, he must think I'm an idiot.

I turn sharply to escape but I'm blocked by Brooke who faces me forward again and nudges me down the stairs further into the auditorium.

"I'm fine." I wave her off and slump down into the seat furthest away from Luke as possible, followed by Brooke. A blush creeps up my neck when Luke raises a quizzical eyebrow with another fucking smirk. He's taking not of my reaction and what…he likes it?

"Oh, hey, Luke!" Brooke says, waving obnoxiously as she pretends to notice our guest for the first time. "Look, Natasha,"— she nudges me with here sharp elbow—"it's Luke. You remember Luke, right? He's staying in the apartment next door to yours."

Fucking hell, I'm going to kill her.

"I can see that, thanks, Skip," I reply through gritted teeth to my captain and soon-to-be-ex-best friend if she keeps this up. Brooke smiles happily like the cat that got the cream, crossing her arms over her chest getting comfortable.

Okay, so, full disclosure, Luke's name has been thrown around the dressing room quite a lot this week. It'll take precisely three minutes for word to get around this room that this is the man I've been simultaneously hating and crushing on in equal measure.

"Nice to see you, Luke," I say with a curt nod as if seeing him is the least exciting part of my week so far when the opposite is more like it.

"Nice to see you too, Natasha," he says in that throaty way he says my name that I haven't been able to get out of my head.

Brooke snorts with laughter, so I look to Bridget for some moral support. She's no better and isn't even trying to hide her glee at the situation.

"Thank you for meeting on such short notice, ladies. I'll keep this brief as I know you want to get out of here," Coach begins. "This is Luke Ramshaw. He's a video game developer and is designing a game based on the Women's Super League."

His gaze is trained on me, so of course he sees the moment I realise I was completely wrong about him. He's not just a deadbeat gamer with no job. Gaming is his job! Not that I know exactly what being a video game developer entails but the way Coach said it made it sound really important.

"The way I understand it, it's like FIFA but exclusively designed for the women's league," Coach continues, looking to Luke who nods his confirmation. "We have struck a deal this morning that in return for his generous sponsorship we will be at his disposal when it comes to assisting him with his work. With this additional investment we can afford to draft in some of the academy players to replace those we've lost in the January transfer window and those we have out on injury. With a little bit of luck, we might actually survive this season. Are there any questions?"

I raise my hand immediately. I have a lot of questions and no idea where to start, so I begin with the obvious.

"What do you mean we'll be at his disposal?"

"Oh, wouldn't you like to know." Debbie, the reserve goalkeeper, sitting on my other side, sniggers, so I jab her in the thigh, shutting her up.

"Luke will be attending training and matches. If he has any questions or needs anything at all I expect you to support him. Any other questions?" A dozen more hands shoot in the air. "Debbie?"

"Are you Natasha's Luke? Because if you are, then I can understand why she hasn't shut up talking about you this week." She laughs, throwing me under the bus.

"Debbie!" I turn in my seat to face her. My face burns so hot I could probably fry an egg on it and Brooke snorts again, failing to disguise it with a cough. "What the actual fuck!?"

"Why don't you take that question, Natasha?" My god he is brazen. "Am I 'your Luke'?" he asks with a mischievous grin. He uncrosses his arms and shoves his hands in his beautifully fitted jeans. All that does is direct my gaze south and to make it worse, he catches me.

"Luke is my temporary neighbour," I answer, quickly averting my gaze. "Is that all, Coach? Can we go now?"

Jesus Christ, I just want to get out of here.

"Does anyone have any more questions?" Coach asks and every single hand in the room flies up. "About the game," she adds, and their arms slowly lower. "Good, as you're already familiar with each other, Natasha, you'll be Luke's point of contact."

"I don't think that's a—"

"It's a wonderful idea," Luke says, locking eyes with me again and the spark we share shoots straight through my body. What the fuck is going on right now?

"Glad that's settled, you can all go now," she says, and just like that, we're dismissed.

CHAPTER SEVEN

Luke

Since the announcement at the academy, I haven't seen much of Natasha. When she's not in a group training session with the team, she's meeting with the physio, in the gym, swimming, mentoring the youth team or any of the other hundred excuses she comes up with to avoid being alone with me.

I'm not sure why. It could be that she's still mad at me for the volume issue or that she's embarrassed I openly flirted with her at the team meeting. What was I thinking?

"Am I your Luke?"

I'm not her Luke, but I would definitely volunteer as tribute given half the chance.

Upon reflection, I didn't exactly make the right impression with her my first day at the academy either. When she asked me what experience I had when it came to women's football, I told her the sport doesn't interest me. It's not true at all. When Mam played I was always in the crowd cheering her on but I didn't want to get into the specifics of why I have issues with women's football these days.

"So why are you designing a game about women's football then if you have no interest?" she'd asked me over coffee with Brooke and Debbie.

I stupidly replied, "Because after the Lionesses' historic win at the Euros, it's what the market is crying out for."

"So, you're doing it for the money," she summarised with judgement in her pretty hazel eyes.

She must think I'm a fucking prick which is why it's a surprise when, on Saturday morning, she knocks on my door.

Her long chocolate brown hair is styled in a French plait that hangs over her shoulder with little wispy strands framing her pretty face. As much as my first impression of Natasha was that she was a little stuck-up, I could barely tear my eyes away from her even as she yelled at me. Call me a masochist or whatever, but I immediately knew I wanted her on a deeply molecular level. Similarly, now, I know I shouldn't, but I'm unable to stop as my gaze travels the length of her body, clad in tight black running leggings and matching sports bra masquerading as a crop top that shows the tanned skin of her toned stomach.

When it comes to this woman, the rational part of my brain doesn't seem to be working any more. I wanted out of this world of women's football. I was happy to leave the pain and heartache behind me ten years ago, and yet, here I am, charging headfirst into the same thing I was running from. I'm fantasising about a woman who is the exact embodiment of everything I tell myself I can't be with.

Did I mention, she thinks I'm a fucking prick?

Silently, Natasha checks me out. Her breath hitches as she works her way slowly and deliberately up my body, starting at my toes, until she reaches my eyes. And she needn't think I don't notice how she lingers at the most important places.

So, maybe she doesn't hate me as much as she'd like to? Interesting.

"Hi." I break the loaded silence between us, smiling knowingly at the blush that creeps up her neck when she realises I caught her checking me out.

"Get your shoes on, we're going for a run," she orders, recovering quickly and planting one hand on her hip.

"*We* as in me and you?" I ask, confused at her sudden change of heart. This is the woman who every day for two weeks left a room when there was a slight chance of her being alone with me.

"Who else would I be talking about?" She looks at me as if I've completely lost the plot. Fuck it, I must have lost the plot because this is so far from what I've come to expect from her. "You run, right? I've seen you go out."

I smirk. So, she's been keeping tabs on me then.

"Yeah, I run. But why do you want to go with me?"

She takes a deep breath. "Bridget said I should offer you an olive bush or something. Apparently, I've been less than welcoming to you and I need to do better."

"Do you mean an olive branch?" I ask, my smile spreading wider. She rolls her eyes at me.

"For fuck's sake, yes."

"Well, with an offer like that, how could I possibly refuse…" I tease.

"I'm trying," she says sincerely. Curiosity gets the better of me, so I cut her some slack.

"Let me get changed."

Less than twenty minutes later, after a silent but surprisingly not awkward drive, Natasha pulls her car into the entrance of Herrington Country Park. I'm hit with a wave of nostalgia at the familiar winding road that leads through the grassy parkland and down to the lakeside where she pulls into a space staring straight ahead at a group of swan's converging on a couple of kids with a bag of feed. I can practically see the cogs turning quickly behind her eyes as she plans her words.

"I'm not good with apologies or talking about feelings and shit, so can we just run for a little bit?" she asks before I can ask if she's okay. It's the first glimpse of vulnerability I've seen in her since we met.

"Sure. It's probably for the best anyway, I always seem to fuck things up when I talk to you." I'm delighted when she lets out a small but genuine laugh. It's a little win I didn't know I needed.

Once we're out of the car, I follow Natasha's lead and let her set the pace, allowing her to remain in control. Maybe if she's comfortable, she'll eventually open up.

I've always liked running outdoors. The sound of our

footsteps pounding the gravel paths mix with the wash of the lake and the animals that inhabit it, providing a calming soundtrack.

After our third or maybe fourth—I've lost count—loop around the lake, Natasha suggests continuing up the path towards Penshaw Hill. She quickens the pace until we're almost sprinting instead of jogging, and by the time we reach the halfway point of the steep incline, she doesn't look too good.

"Stop for a minute." I glance to the sky with my hands on my hips trying to catch my breath. "Are you okay? You look like you're about to throw up." Her cheeks are flushed but at the same time the rest of her face has a pale grey-green tinge to it.

"I'm fine."

"Natasha, it's okay to admit if you're not fine. Cards on the table, my entire body feels like it's on fire," I say, doing my best to encourage her.

"Oh god, you're right," she says with an added groan, giving in and doubling over with her hands on her knees, her breathing heavy and uneven. "I skipped breakfast this morning and, fuck, I feel like I'm dying."

I rub gentle circles on her back in a gesture I hope is comforting and watch as her breathing slowly returns to a steady rhythm.

"Is this okay?" I ask.

"Yeah, it's working. I don't feel like I'm about throw up or pass out anymore." She straightens up once again, the colour slowly returning to her face. "Thank you."

"Do you think you could make it up the last…" I turn to

count but give up and guestimate instead, "thirty, forty steps? We can find a nice spot with a view to sit and talk."

"Okay, let's walk this time though, no running," she jokes with another smile, and the relief that surges through me when I know she's okay almost knocks me off my feet.

CHAPTER EIGHT

Natasha

We reach the wooden steps to Penshaw Monument and Luke offers me his hand. When I take it, another swarm of butterflies flutters in my stomach. Exactly like they did when I knocked on his door this morning and he gave me one of his smirks that says, "I know you're checking me out and I know you like what you see."

"Why are you being so nice to me?" I ask, taking my hand back, shy at his chivalry. I don't deserve it, especially not after the way I've acted towards him.

"Life's too short to hold grudges over petty neighbourly squabbles." He shrugs with a reassuring smile. "I also raised my sixteen-year-old sister when our mam died, so I'm well aware how stubborn women can be."

"Heeey." I nudge him with my shoulder. Although I shouldn't complain when he's right.

Over the past week, after watching him interact with the other girls at the club and taking an interest in what we do, it's clear I got the wrong impression of him. And I don't buy his excuse that he's putting this much effort into this game only for the paycheck. I can see he cares about it deeply. I just can't work out why.

"I'm sorry to hear you lost your mam."

"Thanks, it's been ten years now. I was eighteen when she had a heart attack."

"That must have been tough," I say, seeing him in a completely new light. "What about your dad?"

"He passed when I was two," he explains.

"You don't have to explain, if it makes you uncomfortable." I tell him.

"I guess we're both not great with talking about feelings and shit..." he echoes my earlier statement.

We fall into a comfortable silence, sitting side by side on the north side of the monument. Our feet dangle over the cold stone foundation as we look out across the River Wear towards the industrial green belt of Sunderland. From here we have an unobstructed 360 degree view of the city and in the distance the North Sea twinkles in the sunlight.

I turn my body sideways and rest my back against the thick stone pillar with my legs outstretched on the floor in front of me feeling the tightness settling in. Leaning forward, I grab my feet to stretch out my muscles after our punishing run. I procrastinate a little more before I attempt my apology.

Fuck, this is hard.

"You don't have to talk, but I get the feeling you want to," he prompts, turning his head sideways to look at me. He must have a sixth sense or something.

"I find it extremely difficult to admit that I'm wrong." I take a deep breath. "But I was wrong about you and I'm sorry I judged you. And I don't believe you're doing this solely for the money because I don't think any amount of money is worth sitting listening to Debbie talk for an hour and a half about what it feels like to play football on your period." He laughs at the memory. "I'd really like to start fresh and get to know you and your project properly."

"I'd really like that too," he says. "And I'm sorry, because I judged you too."

"You did?" I ask, curiosity getting the better of me.

"The first time I met you, I thought you were a stuck-up bitch, if I'm honest," he says and a laugh bubbles out from deep within me followed by another and another until we're both laughing uncontrollably.

Passers-by stare at us, but I barely notice because it feels so good to let go of all the shields protecting my emotions. I don't remember the last time I laughed like this over something so small and ridiculous. It's the kind of laugh that as soon as one of us manages to stop, the other finds it even more hilarious and we start the cycle all over again.

"I'm so glad we did this," I say, regaining a sliver of my composure and dabbing away the tears that are leaving streaks down my cheeks. "I feel so much better now."

"I needed that laugh," he says, his eyes shining brightly as he smiles at me, and an unfamiliar warmth radiates from my chest and settles deep within my soul.

"Yeah, me too."

CHAPTER NINE

Luke

Stepping out onto the balcony, coffee in one hand, small watering can in the other, I take in a deep breath of the fresh morning air. The mornings aren't as dark and crisp as they were a few weeks ago now that spring has sprung, and by eight, the sun is already shining above the North Sea in the distance.

I place the mug and watering can on the small wooden table and lift my arms high above my head as I stretch out my back. Sitting in a gaming chair for almost forty-eight hours is not great for the spine.

"Morning, Stanley," I say happily to the plant as I give him a healthy glug of water.

When Natasha and I got home from our run a fortnight ago, I finally gave in and googled her. And I know that sounds stalkerish, but it was in the name of research.

Sort of.

Once I started, I couldn't stop. I fell down a YouTube rabbit hole, watching her play and being interviewed, starting early in her career to as recently as last week. Reading the harsh comments and criticism she has received lately, I'm overwhelmed with the urge to protect her.

I'm overwhelmed by another urge too.

"Who's Stanley?" Natasha's curious voice drifts over from her balcony. I jump in surprise; I hadn't noticed her sitting on the other side of the low wall at her bistro table, sipping her own coffee.

"The plant," I answer, cringing internally.

"Yeah, I know. Hannah talks to him too." She chuckles, standing to lean her elbows on the wall that separates us. She's stunning in the morning, her rich brown hair is tied in a messy bun on top of her head and her skin is smooth, bright and void of any make-up.

In a short space of time her attitude towards me hanging around the academy has changed entirely and each day we spend time together there, she opens up a little bit more, revealing small parts of her personality. I've come to learn she's witty and sarcastic, but also highly self-critical and self-depreciating when it comes to her skill.

I'm sure there's still a lot about her I don't know, but what I do know, I like. And I mean, I *really* like her and I think she likes me too. Now that we're friends, I'm hopeful I'll get to know her better still and see where this goes.

"Oh great, now I look like a crazy plant lady like my little sister!"

"Want to know a secret?" she asks with a sparkle in her eye. "I talk to him too," she whispers loudly, and I laugh effortlessly, like I have every time she says something funny.

"What are your plans for the day?" She looks down at her coffee cup, tucking a stray wisp of hair behind her ear.

"Besides a shower and a shave?" I scratch my beard that's more homeless than *GQ* right now. "Absolutely nothing."

"Does that mean you're free tonight?" She glances at her cup before looking back to me again.

"Yeah."

"We have a game at five and then a few of us are going for drinks after with the rest of our friends, you should come."

Since working with the club, I've not yet attended a game, I've been avoiding it, but looking at Natasha's hopeful eyes the word 'no' doesn't even come into my mind.

"Yeah, that sounds good," I say, and happiness radiates from her. Seeing her reaction makes it easier to ignore the niggle of anxiety the thought of attending a match after so long brings. "Do you have any pre-game rituals?" I lean on the wall next to her, cradling my warm cup in my hands and changing the subject.

"Are you sure you want to open that can of crazy?"

"Come on, it can't be that weird."

"Okay, strap in," she says, as if it's a challenge. "Firstly, I set my alarm for eight. I make a coffee with one sugar, and I sit in that seat right there, she points to the one in the corner behind our connecting wall.

"What if it's bad weather?"

"I wear layers and bring a huge golf umbrella out if there's rain."

"Sounds sensible. Then what?"

"If it's a lunchtime kick off, I'll make a high protein breakfast. Lean bacon, eggs and beans on two slices of wholemeal bread and then I'll snack on a banana about an hour before I play. If it's an evening kick off, I'll have that breakfast and then for lunch I have pasta, chicken, melted cheese triangles and broccoli."

"That sounds reasonable and also disgusting."

She laughs at my comment and another ball of joy bursts in my chest.

"We haven't got to the crazy part yet," she says, and my eyebrows raise questioningly. "I have lucky socks that I must wear from my house to the football ground. I wore them on the day of my professional debut, and we had a great game. I also have to put my trainers on my left foot and then right foot before I leave the house, but when I put my boots on, it's right foot and then left."

"Okay, that is a little strange, I'll give you that."

"I put my gloves on my right hand first and then my left. Because I'm the goalkeeper, I lead the team onto the pitch, and I have to step over the white line with my right foot first. When I get to the goal, I tap the right post with my left foot and hand and then the left post with my right foot and hand before bending over to stretch one last time, placing both palms flat on the goal line in the middle of the posts." She braces herself for my reaction. I'll give her this, it is a bit weird, but Mam was the same before she played so it doesn't surprise me.

Athletes are a breed of their own.

"What happens if you miss a step?"

"Then I'm scared we'll lose, and it affects my confidence and performance," she explains simply. "If you ask a sports psychologist, they'll tell you that pre-game rituals are a placebo and they're probably right, but it still doesn't stop me from doing it."

"Can I join you today?" I ask before adding, "Only if it wouldn't mess with your rituals of course."

"Yeah, I'd like that. I'll get breakfast started. Come over when you're ready," she adds with a happy grin.

CHAPTER TEN

Luke

Twenty minutes later, I've showered and tamed my beard and am sitting at the breakfast bar in Natasha's kitchen, watching as she cooks.

"Have you heard from Hannah lately? Is she having fun?" Natasha asks.

"I spoke to her a few days ago and it sounds like she's living her best life. She's never done anything like this before. She had a big break-up about six months ago so when she first told me she was going, I was concerned to say the least."

"It's natural to be concerned, you're her big brother and you helped raise her. It must be tough seeing her fly the nest so to speak."

"Yeah, it is. But I trust that she's sensible and will make good choices. I just have to remind myself of that."

She places our plates down on the breakfast bar and sits opposite me to eat.

"Do you have siblings?" I ask, and she shakes her head.

"I'm an only child. I have a lot of cousins though."

"Are you close to them?" I ask, and her eyes cloud over for a brief second before she speaks.

"Not really. How do I put it?" She pauses to think. "I'm the black sheep of the family. Unmarried and childless. Gets drunk at family engagements. Huge disappointment and disgrace to the family name."

"You're twenty-six, you've got plenty of time to get married and have kids... you know, if that's what you want."

"Yes. Exactly! I mean, it is something I want one day but maternity rights in football aren't great and so something like that would need to be a strategic choice to get pregnant. And besides that, I've never been with a man I've wanted to marry, anyway... So, until then, it's pointless thinking about it."

Her statement is matter of fact, as though she had the response on the tip of her tongue. Jealousy rears its ugly head at her statement. I really don't want to think about her being with other men. Especially since the past two weeks, or maybe even more, all I've thought about is Natasha being with me.

I knew I was attracted to her even when she didn't like me, but now flirting with her has become a professional sport.

"You're at the height of your career though, your parents must be proud of you."

She lets out a bitter laugh. "They were proud of me when I got my law degree, and then the very next day, I was offered a professional contract playing football at Wearside and took that instead of joining the family business." She looks down at her plate, no longer eating but pushing her food around. "Before then, they tolerated me playing because it was considered a hobby. I think they felt like I was choosing football over them, when really, I was choosing to do something I love instead of working in a job I know I would have hated."

"I'm sorry."

She shrugs. "They've never seen me play, even when I was a kid. My Grandma would take me to training and matches." The sadness in her voice kills me and the urge to protect her from the pain overwhelms me.

"They're missing out." I take her hand and squeeze it revelling in the fact that she doesn't shy away from my physical contact.

"How do you know? You've never seen me play. I could be shit."

"There's this website called YouTube. You type words in the search box and up pops loads of videos."

"You YouTubed me?" she asks with a laugh.

"I did, and I *really* liked what I saw."

The blush I'm obsessed with stains her cheeks a light shade of pink.

"Well, you're in for a treat tonight then, with you there, I'll do my best to put on the performance of a lifetime," she says seductively before returning to her food with a smirk.

"I look forward to it."

Ellie White

CHAPTER ELEVEN

Luke

All those hours spent on YouTube didn't prepare me for what it would be like to watch Natasha play in real life. She's so focused and in control that I watch her constantly instead of the rest of the game. I even miss a Wearside goal because my attention is fixed on her.

I'm taken aback by the confidence she exudes on the pitch when at other times she can be so consumed by her own self-doubt.

"She's really talented," I say to Bridget, sitting next to me in the stand, without peeling my eyes away from the girl who's dominated my every waking thought since I met her, even more so after today.

Spending time with her alone and away from the club today felt intimate, almost like a date. Our conversation flowed easily, we laughed together and joked.

We talked about her career and mine and where we saw ourselves going in the future. I know it's not easy for her to open up to people, so the fact she's slowly letting me into her life

55

makes me wonder if she feels this connection between us too.

After we'd eaten breakfast, we headed next door so I could show her how to play the 'zombie game' she hates so much. I guess she doesn't hate it so much anymore because it was hard to tear her away from it in the end and in that moment, I decided to stop shielding myself from my life. After all, if I want her, this is a package deal.

"Close the gaps, Lasses!" Her voice drifts through the air as she gives instructions to her defenders using exaggerated hand movements. I can't look away.

I don't want to look away because seeing her on the pitch—her cheeks pink from exertion and her shorts pulled up high, exposing more of her long, tanned legs—has my imagination running wild.

"Yeah." Bridget grins, following my eye line to her best friend. From the look she gives me, she knows the direction my thoughts have begun to wander. "She's one of our best. For a while, I was worried about her. She seems happier today though… and so do you."

Before I get a chance to dissect that statement, the whistle blows announcing Wearside Women have won two–nil and all I can think of is getting to the sidelines as quickly as possible.

"Looks like you're our good luck charm," Mel says happily when I arrive at the dugout with Bridget. The team swarm their coach with hugs and cheek kisses, and she laughs throughout like a proud parent.

Natasha is last off the pitch. The excited smile she had a

moment ago is nowhere to be seen as she scans the family and friend's stand.

Is she looking for me? Could I be that lucky?

"Congratulations, you won!" I say proudly, leaning in close from behind so she can hear me. She spins around surprised and a smile lights up her face.

"We won!" she echoes as if she can't quite believe it herself. Laughing happily, she pulls me in for a hug. The scent of her deodorant and the fresh sweat on her skin is intoxicating. I wind my arms around her waist, tugging her closer.

For the longest time I couldn't even picture myself back in the stadium but here I am. And it feels so right.

"I think I need to add something new to my ritual," she says, leaning back slightly but not stepping out of our embrace.

"What's that?" I hold her to me with one hand on her lower back, using the other to tuck a loose strand of hair that's escaped from her plait behind her ear.

"You." Her voice is barely above a whisper, only for me to hear. My stomach flutters with anticipation as I watch her tongue gently wet her lips and the urge to claim her with my mouth overwhelms me.

The only coherent thought I can form is that I need this woman more than I need oxygen in my lungs.

I can't tear my eyes from her mouth. The loud roaring of the stadium drifts into a dull buzz in the background as I move in closer, leaning down ever so slightly. She leans in too, but before I can close the distance and press my lips to hers, Brooke comes bounding over. She wraps us both in a hug before kissing Natasha sloppily on the cheek unaware of what she has interrupted.

Natasha steps back with a shy smile and the absence of her touch makes me ache. As quick as it started, our moment passes.

CHAPTER TWELVE

Natasha

When Luke and I arrive at The Eighteen, a community space/bar hybrid in Sunderland city centre, later that evening, the others are already there waiting for the two of us. Jamie, the owner of the venue, calls us over to take our drinks order and sends us to our usual table in the snug.

Jamie played on the Wearside FC first team until an incident at a game a few years back ended his career. When he opened this place, it became our new local, especially for my friends from the men's team who get to catch up with Jamie and know they aren't going to get swarmed by the patrons. It gives them a sense of normalcy when in the outside world they can barely walk five feet without being recognised and hounded for selfies.

"Everyone, this is Luke Ramshaw. Luke, this is Jordan, Aaron and Bailey," I point them out one by one and they all hold out a hand for Luke to shake.

"Oh, my ever-living fuck!" Aaron says, his jaw slack as he stares at Luke. "You're Zero!"

Luke lets out a chuckle. "Yeah, man, that's me. People in the real world call me Luke though."

"Shut the fuck up! No way!" Bailey says, standing with his mouth wide open. "It is you!"

Luke gives them a humble smile, as if he's used to this reaction from people; I on the other hand, am left stunned. Bailey and Aaron are usually the ones getting fawned over, so to see them so starstruck is plain weird.

"Natasha, do you realise your boyfriend is a living fucking legend?" Aaron says. I look between him and Luke. Neither of us react to the boyfriend comment, I'm too stunned by the fact that my friends are fan-boying hard. "We came to your panel at Game Con Northeast a few months ago! It was fucking wild!"

"What is going on right now?" Brooke asks, her head swinging between the lads like she's watching a tennis match, voicing my question perfectly.

"That zombie game we play all the time that you hate, this guy fucking designed it," Bailey says excitedly, looking at Brooke as if she's a fool. "He's got like eleven million followers on Twitch!"

"I don't hate it," Brooke says, trying to recover, but Luke just laughs. "I'm not great with blood and stuff..."

"Honestly, it's fine, it's not for everyone," he says reassuringly.

"So, you're responsible for hours of torment from these guys then?" Jordan pipes up. "Apparently I suck at your game,

60

and they've never let me live it down."

"They even kicked him out of their apocalypse team," Bridget teases.

"He was dragging us down," Aaron defends his actions.

"We had no choice," Bailey confirms seriously, not a hint of sarcasm in sight.

"And we'd do it again if we had to," Aaron finishes with a firm nod.

Luke laughs, before turning to Jordan. "If you ever want me to show you how to play it, let me know."

"Yes! You two"—Jordan stands and wags his finger between Aaron and Bailey—"are going down!"

I watch Luke from the bar as I collect our drinks and when he turns to grin at me, his green eyes sparkling, my heart skips a beat.

"You and Luke seem to be getting along." Bridget nudges me gently with a knowing smile. "Has anything happened between you two yet?"

"We almost kissed earlier, but we were interrupted."

"Oh my god! When?" she asks excitedly.

"After the game," I respond with a shy smile as I admit it out loud. "Bridget, I think I like him. Like, really like him."

"He's good for you, you should go for it. He couldn't take his eyes off you earlier; it was so adorable!" she says before walking back to the table.

Over the course of the past few weeks Luke and I have gotten closer, that's for sure, I've also shared things with him I couldn't even talk to Brooke or Bridget about. I willingly told him about the pressure I'm under from my parents and my own self-doubts and each day he's helped me navigate them. Now, those negative voices barely even exist anymore.

When I sit down next to him again, I move closer, barely leaving any room between us. He smiles down at me knowingly, then reaches over and takes my hand. He rests it on the table and threads his fingers through mine. Claiming me for the world to see. And I couldn't be happier.

CHAPTER THIRTEEN

Natasha

"I had a really good night," Luke says when we reach my front door, my hand still safely tucked away in his just like it has been all night. No one batted an eyelid to the shift in our relationship.

"Me too." My heart rate increases rapidly and my stomach flutters as he looks at me with those beautiful green eyes again.

He places his palm flat on my waist as he leans in to kiss my cheek and, oh god, even though it's just a small peck, it's delightful. He lingers for a moment, running his nose along my cheekbone slowly, and my hands tremble with anticipation.

The smell of his aftershave hovers between us, a scent I could pick out a mile away now having spent so much time in his presence.

"Luke?" I whisper, gripping his shoulders as though frightened he'll disappear.

"Yeah, Nat?" His voice is low and hoarse, and I love it so much I let out a sound that sounds suspiciously like a whimper. It's the first time he's shortened my name to Nat and I like the way it sounds in his low tone.

I turn my face ever so slightly, lining up our lips perfectly with barely a centimetre between us. He nudges my nose affectionately with his as he brings his hand up to cup my jaw and I let out a tiny gasp.

"I'm so glad I met you," I say breathily, my voice barely above a whisper.

His heart's beating fast beneath his soft t-shirt against my hand. His body is warm against my palm and all I can think about is how fantastic it would feel to be lying next to him with nothing between us.

"Me too," he says.

When his lips caress mine, I'm floating on air. He kisses me slowly and thoroughly, so much so, my entire body melts against him.

Never have I been so turned on by a kiss. Never has a kiss made me desperate for so much more, and he knows it, because when he pulls back to look at me, the smile he gives me is downright wicked.

Hooking my arms around his neck, I pull him back to me, parting my lips. When his tongue tangles with mine even more sparks fly and it's like a dam breaks inside us, allowing our desperation and desires to take control. He pushes me against the hard surface of my front door and I moan into his mouth, unable to keep quiet any longer as my fantasies play out in real life. The throbbing between my legs intensifies and I try to climb him, so he helps me by hitching my leg up around his hips. His hard bulge presses exactly where I crave. My desperate cry meets his tortured

64

groan. Although this is by far the hottest make-out I've ever had, it's nowhere near enough.

"I want you," I moan when his lips move to caress the tender skin of my neck. "Luke, I need you."

"I want you too, Natasha," he says through kisses. "It's been so fucking long that I've thought about doing this."

"Call me Nat." I gasp when he grinds against me once more and he gives a throaty laugh. "I liked it."

Recognising that we're dry humping in the corridor, I fumble with my bag to get my keys, turning away from him towards the lock. He stands behind me, pressing his hard body into me; his erection digs into the base of my spine and his hand slides lower, over my hips to the hem of my dress, following the line around until he reaches the inside of my thigh.

"I need you, Nat." His other hand drifts over my breast finding the already stiff peak of my nipple and gently strokes it through the fabric of my dress.

"Oh, god," I moan, my head dropping back against his shoulder when he teases across my underwear.

When he realises I'm so distracted that I've stopped trying to open the door, he reaches over me and pushes it open with a clatter, walking me inside.

"Ever since I saw you in this little black mini dress all I've thought about is stripping you out of it," he says in my ear and more sparks my down my spine.

"Do it." I relinquish all control to him. "Please do it."

Slowly, he peels down the zip at the back, letting the light material of the dress drop to the floor.

"Fuck," he breathes as all I'm left in is a minuscule black lace thong and my heels. I glance over my shoulder to see him taking me in, his eyes almost black with need. "Nat, you look incredible."

He kisses me again, allowing his hands to roam all over me, skimming my stomach until he reaches my breasts. He turns me in his arms so I'm looking up at him as he toys with my nipples again.

With one hand on his neck as we kiss, I palm against his jeans with the other, slowly unbuttoning the fly, and push them down to his ankles so he can step out of them. Somehow, he manages to throw his t-shirt aside and manoeuvre me down onto the couch where he towers over me.

Fuck, he looks like my wildest fantasy come to life.

"So many times, I've dreamed about this." He strokes over the lace that barely covers me. "So many times, I've fantasised about how you'd taste and the noises you'd make."

"You don't need to fantasise about it anymore. I'm all yours," I say, grinding myself against him.

He slips beneath the fabric, gliding his thick fingers over the sensitive flesh as if he has a map of my body telling him where my favourite parts are.

I cry in protest when he takes his fingers back, but then he sucks them into his mouth with a contented sigh. It's quite possibly the sexiest thing I've ever seen.

Crushing his mouth against mine, our kiss resumes. He

drops his hand to meet the heat radiating between my thighs. Finally he pushes two long thick fingers deep inside me. I cry out, the sound stilted by his kiss as he strokes me from the inside. I can barely think straight. All I can focus on is how I never want to go another day in my life without this. Without him.

My orgasm builds quickly, but I'm not ready yet. "Wait, I'm too close!" I cry.

"I want to taste you." He withdraws his fingers and rests back on his heels. He's straining against his boxers, so I grip and rub him through the fabric. He leans into my touch, grinding against my hand with a deep groan.

Hooking his fingers in the waistband of my thong, he peels it slowly down my legs before effortlessly picking me up and flipping us so that he's lying on the sofa beneath me. He nudges my legs and I crawl above him. His mischievous eyes meet mine as he places his tongue where I need him most. I cry with pleasure as his lips seal around my clit.

Okay, Luke beneath me as I writhe from his touch, is the sexiest thing I've ever seen.

I grip the back of the couch with one hand and bury the other into his hair, tugging gently as he devours me. He licks and sucks softly and slowly, alternating with his fingers as if he's savouring the moment as much as I'm trying to.

He urges me on with a firm hand on my hips so I'm grinding against his mouth. This only drives me faster towards my release and judging by the encouraging sounds of pleasure coming from him, he knows exactly what he's doing to me.

"Oh, Luke," I moan loudly as I completely shatter against him. My climax hits and my body spasms on top of him. "Yes!" I cry again and again, riding it out.

He stays with me, licking and toying with me gently as my orgasm ravages through my body, leaving me limp and dazed.

CHAPTER FOURTEEN

Luke

Post-orgasm Natasha is probably the most relaxed I've ever seen her. Her neck and breasts are flushed pink and her eyes are glassy and satisfied. She's unsteady on her feet as she stands, laughing as she sways to take off her forgotten heels before climbing back on to my lap and kissing me slowly.

"Watching you fall apart like that is my new favourite thing," I say against her mouth as we kiss.

"I can think of something else you might enjoy." She rubs herself against my erection. My hand slides down her back and over her bum, loving how soft she feels against my palm. I run my fingers over her from behind and she gasps again as I focus on slowly teasing her clit.

"Is this okay?" I ask, aware that only seconds ago she was limp in my arms.

She gasps again. "God yes. I need more. I need you," she begs as I push a finger inside her. "Please," she adds on a gasp.

Carrying her in my arms, I stride to her bedroom as quickly as my feet can carry us. I lay on her bed, and she shuffles backwards until she's propped up on her elbows, watching me with her legs spread wide, waiting for me.

I pull down my boxers and crawl towards her until I'm settled between her legs, the head of my dick rubbing against her clit.

"Condom?" I ask.

"I'm on the pill and I'm clean," she says. "But if you'd prefer, there's some in the drawer."

"I'm clean too, but I don't want to pressure you," I reply.

"I want to feel all of you," she says, and this time when I kiss her, it isn't frantic or messy. It's tender and unhurried because we both know how much this means to us.

"I've never done it without," I tell her honestly, rubbing the head of my dick across her wet heat so I'm lined up with her opening.

"Me neither, but I trust you. I feel safe with you."

"You are safe with me, and I trust you too."

I kiss her as I sink into her slowly. She's tight and perfect, and I'm pretty sure I'm ruined for anyone else now.

I pause to take control of my breathing before I completely fuck this up, pulling out of her and slowly sliding in a little further each time until I'm buried deep inside. Each thrust of my hips draws out the most delicious sounds from her.

"Yes! Fuck, yes!" The sounds of our bodies colliding and her encouraging cries spur me on until I can feel my own release building.

I sit back to switch up the angle, bringing my thumb down

between us to circle her clit as I watch her writhing beneath me. Her back arches and she cries out again.

"Come for me, Nat, I want to feel you," I growl, barely hanging on.

"Luke, yes! Oh god, yes, I'm coming!" she cries out, and that's the end of me. When I feel her clench around me in climax, my body tenses from the tips of my toes to the top of my head until I burst inside her with a guttural growl. Each hard thrust I give her, she tightens and squeezes more from me until neither of us can take the sensation anymore.

She reaches for me, her arms winding around my neck, and I lower my mouth to hers, kissing her softly as we both come down from our high.

CHAPTER FIFTEEN

Natasha

Luke stirs next to me as I slide his arm off me and climb out of bed to grab my phone that's been vibrating on the kitchen island for the past few minutes. It's been five days since Luke and I got together and any spare moment we have when we aren't at the academy, we've spent in my bed or next door as Luke attempts to teach me to play his game. Truth be told, I'm not very good at it.

I'm so blissfully happy with how things are going right now, the girls on the team thought I'd had a lobotomy.

On Saturday we won against Middlesbrough four–nil, clawing back some much-needed goal difference and awarding us another three points. Thankfully the teams around us in the table didn't do as well and so instead of sitting at the bottom of the relegation zone, we're just above it.

Mam's name appears next to three missed calls and I'm hit with a wave of nausea as I call her back immediately, not knowing what awaits me.

"Oh, so you are alive?" she asks sarcastically when she picks up my call on the first ring. "That's good to know."

72

"Is everything okay?"

"I could ask the same of you, you're the one avoiding your family."

"Yeah, I've been busy with that project I was telling you about." I had mentioned it to my parents and may have used it as an excuse not to go around for tea on Saturday. It's not like it's a lie or anything. I did spend the day and the evening with Luke, and we worked on the game as well as him showing me how to play other games he's worked on.

We also had a lot of earth-shattering sex, but I won't be telling her that.

"Are you gracing us with your presence this weekend?"

"I'm sorry, I don't know. We'll have to see how it goes this week, we're still not finished with the game and need all hands on deck." This time it's true. Luke tells me he's applying the code for the visual effects and graphic design this week and I want to be there with him to see it come to life.

"So, when will I get to see my daughter?"

"You could always come to the stadium and watch me play."

"Don't be ridiculous, I'd never get your dad through those doors."

"Not even to see me?" My voice falters on the last word because I

know the answer to that question.

Luke strolls into the room and sits on one of the bar stools in my kitchen, pulling me to him, wrapping his arms around my waist and silently pressing his lips to my shoulder.

"Actually, Mam, don't answer that. I have to go. I love you." Before she has a chance to react, I hang up and throw my phone onto the side and slide into Luke's waiting arms. A tear slips out and down my cheek as he strokes my hair.

"It's okay, let it out. I've got you." The comfort of his hand on my back and his supportive words release the floodgates. He holds me tight as I cry. No judgement, just soothing sounds and caresses.

"Sorry you had to see that," I say when I eventually pull myself together. "I should get ready. We've got a date."

"Nat, we don't have to go if you'd rather stay here?"

"I want to go," I say honestly, kissing him softly on the lips. "I was looking forward to it before she called."

CHAPTER SIXTEEN

Natasha

Where are we going?" I ask as Luke drives us through an industrial estate on the outskirts of Durham a little while later.

"I don't want to ruin the surprise," he says with an air of mystery that immediately makes me smile.

I recognise a few other cars in the car park when we arrive at our secret destination. Why are Brooke and Bridget here? And is that Debbie's car?

Luke climbs out and quickly jogs around to my side to open the door. There's a sign fixed on the side of the corrugated iron unit that reads Durham VFX. From spending so much time with Luke, I'm proud to say I understand what VFX stands for.

"Are we going to see the game?" I turn to him and grip his arm in excitement.

"Not exactly, but it is something equally as fun. Come on." He takes my hand and leads me to the entrance.

When we enter the building through the heavy glass doors, we emerge into a small cold office. There's no one else around apart from a boy, who can't be much older than sixteen, sitting at the reception desk with a gaming headset on. When he spots us, he tosses the headset aside as if it's caught on fire and jumps out of his seat.

"It's such an honour," he says, vigorously shaking Luke's hand and not paying me an ounce of attention. The boy is visibly trembling as he looks up at him with big puppy dog, love-heart eyes.

"It's nice to meet you," Luke begins, glancing at the boy's name badge, "Ryan."

"Oh my god," the boy swoons, like actually fucking swoons. After the handshake lasts a little longer than what is comfortable, Luke carefully extracts his hand from Ryan's vice-like grip and flexes his knuckles as if they're in pain.

"We'll head on through, mate?" Luke points to another heavy set of glass doors.

"Studio six."

Luke leads me towards them, leaving a stunned Ryan to go back to his game.

"I shit you not, I just met Zero and he knew my fucking name," I hear him bragging down his headset. "I'm not lying!" he whines, and thankfully we make it through the double doors before Luke is called back to prove it to whoever is on the other end of the headset.

"I have so many questions!" I'm almost bursting with excitement at this new development. "Are you famous?"

"Define famous."

"Well firstly, Aaron and Bailey were pretty starstruck." I

hold my hand up to count. "Then that kid almost wet himself meeting you and bragged about it to his friends on his headset."

"In the gaming community, I suppose you could say I have a following. Or at least, Zero has a following. I'm just the guy behind the online persona." He shrugs as if it isn't a huge deal.

"Wow! My—" I cut myself off before I call Luke my boyfriend because even though the others made jokes about it the other night, we're yet to have that talk. "You're famous," I amend.

"I have been known to pull in a good crowd at a gaming convention," he brags sarcastically.

"I bet you do, you're a hot nerd!"

"Is that your type?" He stops in the hallway and pulls me so I fall into his chest.

"My type is you." I step on my tiptoes to kiss him.

"Oh good, you're here!" Bridget says, stepping out of the studio at the end of the corridor, ending our conversation. "They're all ready," she adds with a cheeky smirk, and I realise it's the first time I've seen the happy mischievous side of her in a long time.

"I can't wait for you to see this." Luke tugs me forwards with a skip.

As soon I cross the threshold into the large open studio, I double over, laughter bursting out of me. All the girls, except Bridget, who's dressed in one of her usual figure-hugging dresses, are wearing some sort of Lycra body suit with tiny fluorescent tabs stuck to them.

"I wouldn't laugh just yet, Natasha Borthwick," Luke says, standing close behind me with his arm wrapped around my chest, kissing my cheek. "You're the star of the show."

CHAPTER SEVENTEEN

Luke

Watching the team mess around in their motion capture suits all afternoon is easily the funniest part of this project so far. They leap around the room with various footballs, trying to outdo each other with complicated tricks and fancy footwork, showing off and competing with one another while they all laugh happily.

Nat has fun too, which I'm relieved about. I had worried this morning that the confrontation with her mam would sour the day for her, but seeing her now, smiling that big, beautiful smile that lights up her face, I needn't have worried.

"Okay, ladies, that's us done for the day," I announce, and the women let out a collective groan.

"But we're having so much fun," Brooke whines. "Can we have five more minutes to take some selfies?"

"Sure." I shake my head with a laugh when they all cheer.

"You too, Luke," Nat calls, grinning over at me. I'm not going to lie, she makes this tight-fitting VFX suit look incredible. Sighing sarcastically, pretending it's a chore, I make my way over to where they are gathered. They all know I'm having as much fun as they are.

After a few minutes of posing for pictures, they all make their way through to the changing area, except Nat, who joins me at the computer set up.

"Here, take a few of us." Nat hands me her phone. She wraps her arms around my neck, leaning over me from behind as I stay seated in my chair. Her hair is loose and hangs over my shoulder, the comforting smell of her shampoo enveloping me.

She smiles first at the camera, and then at me as I snap a few photos of the two of us. I can't deny we look good together even if she does look a little bit ridiculous right now.

"I need to get this off, I'm sweating." She pulls the front zip down to her waist so the suit can slide over her shoulders. She ties the arms in a knot around her waist, her top half covered in a black sports bra one of the girls brought for her to wear today. Whoever brought it, I owe them one.

I spin in my chair to face her, swiping her legs from under her and catching her across my lap. She gasps as she grins at me.

"Smooth!" she says as my lips meet hers in a passionate kiss.

"It's a shame this place has cameras, otherwise I'd have gotten you out of that suit by now."

"Can we borrow it for later?" she says with a cheeky smile, and I laugh.

"It wouldn't last two minutes if I had you alone in your bedroom wearing it."

She kisses me hungrily again.

"I should go get changed or the girls might think we are up to no good in here," she says, but making no attempt to climb off my knee.

"Brooke is going to take you home this afternoon, I hope that's okay. I have to stay and sort through this footage while I have the studio and the technicians booked."

"Okay, don't stay too late. You need to rest too." She looks up at me with concern, running her hands through my hair and down my neck. I melt into her touch and let out a relaxed moan as my head lolls to the side.

"You're incredible, Nat. You know that right?"

"I'm glad you think so." She's trying to sound like she's joking, but I know her well enough now to see when she's self-conscious.

"I mean it." I stroke her neck and tilt her face to look at me again. "Before we started this, I was stuck in the same place I'd been for years. Even though this game means more to me than anyone will ever know, I had no drive, no motivation, no inspiration. The second I met you something in me clicked. I would never have gotten this far without you."

"Thank you," she says shyly.

"I wish you could see yourself like I do. You're beautiful and kind and a true inspiration. I wish you could see the way you build up and inspire those little girls who wait around after a match to talk to you. I wish you could truly grasp the way they admire you. You're their role model, Nat. You're changing their life simply by being true to your- self, and I know not everyone in your life understands that. They don't see the real you. But I do. I see it all. I just thought you should know."

She swipes away a rogue tear from her cheek.

"Thank you," she whispers, kissing me. "I needed to hear that."

"Whatever you need, Nat. I'll move heaven and earth to give it to you."

CHAPTER EIGHTEEN

Luke

The light drizzle that began early this morning has evolved into a torrential downpour. From my usual seat in the stand, I can see Nat is soaked to the bone. Her hair is drenched, she's constantly wiping the rain that drips from her nose and there are water droplets running down her body.

"Bridget, at what point does the match get cancelled?" I ask as the rain comes in sideways.

"Oh, they've played in much worse conditions than this. I wouldn't worry," she says, which doesn't help at all because I am worried. It's not even half-time and the girls already look exhausted from trying to stop themselves slipping constantly on the mud, and although it's now approaching summer, the wind still has a chill to it. "It looks like it's expected to be sunny in the second half. This will pass," Bridget says, putting her phone back in her pocket after checking her weather app and returning her attention to the pitch to shout at a decision the referee has made in favour of the opposition.

Since Natasha and I got together a few weeks back, I've

been to all her games and the anxiety is always there. It starts the second she walks away from me in the stadium to get ready for the match and doesn't go away again until she's back by my side. Obviously, I've hidden this anxiety from her, I don't want to put any more pressure on her than she's already under.

I turn back to watch the match, which is currently nil–nil, unconvinced that the dark clouds above are ever going to clear. Although Mam passed away in autumn, the conditions are eerily alike. The dark clouds and the rain, the team they're playing against, and the fact Natasha is playing in the same position she did.

Less than five minutes later, one of the Durham City players sprints with the ball towards Nat's goal. She's fast and our defenders have trouble keeping up with her with the condition of the field, slipping and stumbling as they try to close the distance.

It all happens s quickly. As she shoots towards the bottom right corner, Nat dives to the floor, pushing the ball away with her outstretched hands and saving the goal. But when I'd expect her to come to a stop, she doesn't, she continues to slide on her shoulder until her tiny frame collides heavily with the post, shaking her like a ragdoll.

Even from the stands, I can hear her yelp as she hits it and then there's nothing, nothing at all. No movement, no talking, nothing.

The world around me throbs in my ears, the sounds of the stadium non-existent as panic builds in my chest and I watch the medics run to the girl I love, lying lifeless between the goal posts.

Everything else might as well not exist because the only thing I'm aware of is the thumping heartbeat in my chest.

"Luke, Luke, are you okay?" I can only just make out Bridget's voice through the brain fog. "Luke?" she shouts, finally getting through to me as the noise rushes back to my ears and I return to the moment.

"She... she's not moving. Why isn't she moving?"

Bridget stands to look over the crowd that are now murmuring between themselves as they watch.

"Come on, I can't take you to the touchline, but... look they've got her onto her knees and Debbie is getting ready to go out, so they're taking her off. Let's go to the changing rooms, they'll be taking her there."

Bridget drags me by my arm, down the row and towards the stone steps that lead out of the stadium. Numbly, I follow, not really paying attention to my surroundings, instead relying on muscle memory alone.

When we reach the changing room, we're held outside. It's agony, not knowing. It's agony not being able too see her for myself, to see that she's okay with my own eyes.

The first thing I see when I eventually do enter the room is Nat, sitting on the cold wooden slats of the bench, being fussed over by medics and some of the coaching staff. She smiles up at me when she notices me standing frozen in the door frame. I wish I felt relief, but I don't because my focus is on the fact that, for a moment, I thought she could be dead.

"Luke, you look terrible," she says, looking between me

and Bridget. "You're so pale, what's wrong?"

"You're okay?" I ask, rooted to the spot. She's soaking wet and winces when the medic moves her arm.

"I'm sore but luckily nothing is dislocated or broken so I'll be fine in a few days." She smiles, but it doesn't reach her eyes. "Are you okay?" she asks again, and I nod unconvincingly.

"You're going to have a canny bruise," one of the medics says to her with a chuckle and Nat laughs too until she looks over to me again.

"I'll be done in five minutes. Can you take me home, Luke?" she asks me carefully, as if she knows I'm close to breaking down.

"Yeah, I'll wait outside for you to get your things." I need to get the fuck out of here before the room closes in on me completely.

CHAPTER NINETEEN

Natasha

Despite the agonising pain in my right shoulder, I dress as quickly as I can, without even bothering to shower. I need to find Luke.

Bridget told me about his panic in the stands and I want to get to him as quickly as possible and reassure him that I really am okay. These things happen; it's why we have Debbie as a substitute.

When I reach the car park outside the stadium, Luke is waiting for me by his car, his shoulders slumped and his hands stuffed into the pockets of his jeans. He looks exhausted, as if he's not slept for weeks.

He lifts his head and smiles at me when I approach, but it's not his usual bright and happy smile, it's forced. Even the kiss he gives me as he opens my car door is forced, and unease sweeps over me, something is wrong.

I watch as he climbs in next to me, buckling his seat belt and starting the engine avoiding my gaze completely.

"You're sure you're okay?" he asks when he pulls out of the car park onto the main road that leads back to our building.

"Yeah, honestly, I'm fine. It'll probably ache for a few days and bruise but apart from that, it's all good," I say, but he doesn't reply, he just nods tightly, so I continue trying to reassure him. "It happens all the time, so it isn't anything to worry about. It's not even the worst injury I've had."

I'm aiming for reassuring, as if brushing this pain off will help matters, but as soon the words tumble from me, I know I've said something wrong. He grips the steering wheel so hard his knuckles turn white as though he's doing his best not to burst out of his skin. For the remainder of the journey there's an awkward silence between us. No matter how many times I try to start a conversation with him, I get one-word answers or nothing at all, and by the time we get home, I'm a ball of anxiety.

"Luke, please talk to me," I say, as he places my football bag down on the floor by my door.

I can't take the stilted atmosphere hanging between us anymore.

Instead of answering, he closes the distance between us, taking me in his arms very carefully, and kisses me deeply as though his emotions are being imprinted on my soul. I lean into him, giving everything I have right back to him, hoping it's enough.

It doesn't take long to truly understand the meaning behind this kiss, and it's not one I like, because it feels a lot like a goodbye. When it comes to a natural end, it's my turn to panic.

"Natasha," he says, stepping back.

"Don't," I say, already knowing where this is going. I'm

losing him. "Please don't do this. Don't walk away from us."

He takes my hands that are clinging onto him, removes them from his chest and squeezes them before letting them go.

"I have to," he says, he drops his eyes, unable to look at me anymore.

"Why, why do you have to?" I say, my voice louder than I anticipated. It shocks both of us but all I can focus on is keeping him.

"Because... Fuck, this is hard." He paces the room, putting space between us.

"Please talk to me. It doesn't need to be hard; we can talk it through together. Whatever is going on it'll be okay. Trust me, please," I beg him, my desperation clear as day.

I can't understand how just this morning we were waking up together, making love, eating breakfast, travelling to the game. And now...this. It's not right.

"Seeing you out there, lying lifeless between the same goalposts as she did, I felt like that scared eighteen-year-old boy again!" he stumbles over his words, any trace of self control he was clinging onto has snapped. "My instinct after I saw that you were semi-okay was to be angry at myself for not protecting you better and demand that you give all this up, because I can't lose another woman I love on a football pitch."

"Luke..." I put aside the fact he's just told me he loves me and focus on the important part. A part I should have figured out a long time ago. "Lauren Ramshaw...she's your mam."

"Yeah," he says, and it all makes sense now. His

connection to Coach who played alongside her for most of her career. His purpose for designing a game based on women's football when he outright told me he had no interest in the sport.

I've been in his sisters apartment dozens of times, surely there will be pictures there that I've missed.

How did I miss this?

"Luke, we can talk about it." I reach for him, trying to provide some sort of comfort but deep down I know this is over.

I remind him of her. She was my mentor, she had a direct influence on me growing up so of course there are elements of my skill that mirror hers.

And he's right, I laid there between the same goalposts as she did for a few agonising minutes as I struggled to come around after such a brutal hit.

"It's not about that. I know I have issues when it comes to my mam's death that I need to resolve, and one day I will. But what I hated today, was my reaction. I was so quick to want to pull you away from a career you love for completely selfish reasons." He steps away from me closer to the door. "You deserve so much better than that, so much better than I can give you."

Tears fall down my cheeks thick and fast. "Luke, please don't go."

"I'm sorry, I can't do this anymore. It's over."

I want to fight, I want to shake him until he sees sense but his mind is made up. There's nothing more for me to do than watch as he walks out of my flat for the last time, leaving me heartbroken and alone.

Bridget and Brooke find me an hour later, crumpled and crying uncontrollably into a pillow on the floor of my living room. I don't have to tell them what happened, they already know. I assume Luke called and sent them to me.

They pick me up and help me into the bathroom where they force me to shower away all the grass and dirt still caked to my legs and arms from the match. If it was up to me, I'd have stayed in the same position for god knows how long.

I go through the motions of washing my body and my hair, drying and dressing myself, telling myself I'll feel better when I'm done.

But even when I'm sitting on the sofa, dressed in the PJs I wore when I confronted him all those weeks ago, I don't feel better at all.

"I'll fucking castrate him if I ever see him again!" Brooke shouts loudly, with the hopes he hears her through the thin walls. "Slowly with a rusty butter knife."

"Brooke," Bridget warns her looking between us but I don't respond.

Bridget crouches down next to me where I lay on my sofa.

"What can we do?" Her voice is as calming as ever but it has no affect on my mood.

"I just want to go to bed," I tell her. I pick myself up and shuffle towards my bedroom door. The girls will let themselves out.

"There has to be something we can do," Brooke looks at

me helplessly.

"He has his reasons, Brooke. And there's nothing any of us can do to change his mind."

CHAPTER TWENTY

Luke

"Well, this is a lovely surprise," Hannah says as I let her into her flat a week later. She landed at Newcastle airport an hour ago with a golden tan and her bright curly hair impossibly blonder. "The plants seem to be thriving."

"I took care of them exactly as you said." I'm surprised Hannah hasn't pulled me on my attitude yet but I know she won't let me wallow in my sadness for too long. I know my sister better than I know myself. She's biding her time.

"Tea?" I ask.

"I would love a cup! I don't know what it is, but Aussie tea just isn't the same," she says, and I make my way to the kitchen to put the kettle on buying myself a few more minutes. I catch my reflection in the microwave and cringe. Even though it's a distorted image, I can see how dark my eyes are. I've not slept much this past week. It's hard to sleep alone especially since the one thing I need most in this world is within touching distance. Instead, I've done all I can to distract myself which includes gaming all hours of the night and day.

It'll be easier to get over her when I'm back in my own house. At least, that's what I tell myself.

"So," she asks when I return with two steaming cups. "Are you going to tell me why you're so miserable? Or should I annoy it out of you instead?"

"I'm not miserable, Han."

"Really, you fooled me!" She sighs heavily. "I know heartbreak when I see it, Luke."

She's right, this is heartbreak. As soon as I pushed Nat away, my heart shattered into a thousand pieces, ripping me to shreds from the inside out. Everything inside me wanted me to turn around and take it all back, but the complete panic and loss of control at the stadium scared me. I couldn't lose her to another accident and I couldn't keep her, knowing I was seconds away from demanding she give it all up for me.

"It's for the best," I say, offering her no more than that.

"Best for who? You or her?"

"Both of us," I answer simply.

"Mmm-hmm, and what does Natasha think of this?"

"How do you know it's Nat?"

"Because every time we spoke while I was away, you'd bring her name up. Even if we were talking about something completely unrelated, you'd find a way to mention her. I could hear the happiness radiating from you every time. You talk about her like she's the sunshine and you're the starving plant coming to life after a bleak winter."

"Does everything need to be about plants?" I deflect.

"Tell me what you did to ruin this."

I let out a heavy breath. If there's anyone in this world that will understand why I did this, it'll be my sister.

"She got hurt in a game and I... I completely lost it." Even that feels like an understatement. Had a breakdown and ruined my life might be a better choice of words.

"She plays in goal, doesn't she?" Hannah says, understanding in her soft eyes.

"It was exactly the same. Same pitch, same goal, same opposition, same weather conditions." I sit on the sofa, rub my hands over my face and groan as I massage my aching temples. "As soon as I saw she was okay, the thought ran through my mind that I needed her to quit. That I needed her to give up everything for me."

"But you didn't say it, did you?" she asks, and I shake my head.

"Every relationship I've been in has ended because I'm overbearing and overprotective and I didn't even love those women." But I love Nat, and that terrifies me.

"Luke, this was a random, intrusive thought in the heat of the moment. Like when you think, I wonder what would happen if I swerve my car on the motorway or you're holding a baby and think, I wonder what would happen if I dropped it. There's no way you meant it and I don't believe for one second, you'd actually ask her to give it all up for you."

"I can't risk losing her like we lost Mam. I couldn't live through that again."

"Luke, for fuck's sake, you're an idiot! You've already lost her because you pushed her away. But that's not going to stop you loving her or caring about her. Those worries are a trauma response and will always be there, whether you're together or not, so why not choose to be happy, go to therapy and work through this as a couple? She'll understand and if she loves you like you love her I can guarantee she'll stick by your side as you work this all out."

I don't answer her question, I don't think she actually needs an answer because we both know it would have been the sensible thing for me to have done in the first place. Not only that, but it's what I want to do; it's what you do when you're in love, you work together through everything.

Fuck, Hannah's right, I am such an idiot.

"I don't even know if she'll give me another chance." I jump to my feet.

"There's only one way to find out, go and find her."

CHAPTER TWENTY-ONE

Natasha

Reality hits when I hear Luke bringing Hannah home from the airport.

He's laughing and joking in the corridor as he carries her bags in, and honestly, the fact that he sounds fine, as if he didn't shatter my heart into a million pieces a week ago, hurts like fuck.

There is no way I can stay here listening to that through the wall so I pull on my running shoes and grab my keys, doing the only thing I can think of that will help, and drive to my favourite running spot.

It's still bright out when I reach Herrington Country Park, although the temperature has definitely dropped as the sun begins to set. It doesn't bother me much because, by the time I finish my first loop around the lake, I'm sweating.

Somewhere in the very back of my mind I know I should be taking it easy given my recent clash with a large metal goalpost, but I can't help myself. I chase relief by pounding my feet into the pavement and pushing harder than ever, letting the burn of my lungs distract me from the pain coursing through the rest of my body.

I only allow myself to come to a stop when I reach the top of Penshaw Hill. Every fibre of my body is screaming at me as I double over, shadowed by Penshaw Monument. My body trembles and I drop to my knees on the grass. It's the only thing I can do to stop my legs giving out completely.

My lungs burn as I fight for breath. My vision blurs.

Why the fuck did I think this was a good idea?

Pressing the heels of my palms to my eyes, a sob escapes me.

I can't do this anymore. I can't pretend I'm not in pain, both physical and emotional.

"Nat?" His voice in my mind is so clear it breaks through the sounds of my ragged heartbeat throbbing in my ears.

"Nat?" his voice says again. "Are you okay? Are you hurt?" Luke places his hand on my back, rubbing comforting circles like he did the last time we were here together.

Luke!

I look up, shocked to see he's here. He's standing in front of me. This is not a figment of my depressing imagination.

He's here!

But why?

"You're... You're here," I say, which is ridiculous. I swipe the tears from my eyes and cheeks so I can see him clearer.

The sudden movement jars my shoulder and I wince.

He helps me to my feet. I want to go to him. I want to

throw myself into his arms, kiss him senseless and delete the past week from my memory, but I stop myself and take a step back.

He broke up with me, he's the reason I'm here punishing myself for falling in love in the first place.

As we stand facing one another, I take him in. He looks as terrible as I feel. Dark shadows ring his eyes as though he's not slept, his hair is messy and his beard is longer than usual.

"Are you okay?" he asks glancing from my tear-stained cheeks to my shoulder.

"Why did you come here?" I ask.

He doesn't even hesitate. "Because I fucked up, Nat. When I came to the club, the last thing I wanted to do was fall for a footballer after what happened to Mam. But then you burst into my life and shook things up in a way I didn't know I needed. You were feisty and sarcastic and passionate and I fell in love with you in no time at all. I've never had a long-term relationship. I've never met anyone I've wanted to commit to beyond a few dates because I was scared to let myself love and then lose like I did her. I was there the day she died. I watched along with the fans, and the world dropped out from beneath me. I know it's not an excuse, but it explains why I freaked out…"

Although my breathing has returned to normal, tears stream down my cheeks as I digest this information.

"When I saw you get hurt in the exact same place, it triggered my trauma, and I didn't know how to handle it. I should have stayed and talked it through with you and not a minute goes by that I don't hate myself for leaving you that night. If I could go back and change it, I would in an instant. Nat, life without you is like living without the sun, it's dark and cold and I don't want to live like that anymore. I don't want to just exist. I want to be with you, it's where I belong."

A mix of emotions swirls through me. I want to protect him, I want to throttle him, I want to let him back in. He watches me carefully assessing my reaction to his words.

Finally, after a few silent beats, I step closer to him, finding his embrace and winding my arms around his neck. My shoulder twinges again but I push through because feeling him press up against me and hold me tight is worth the pain.

"Promise me, you won't hold anything back from me again. I want to be the person you come to no matter what."

"I promise." He buries his face in my neck as the tension I've been carrying dissolves, my fingers finding his soft hair at the nape of his neck.

"I love you, Luke," I tell him for the first time.

He pulls back and his eyes meet mine. There's relief there and a spark of something else too.

"Fuck, I'm so relieved to hear you say that." I laugh softly as he cups my face but it trails off when his expression turns from elated to serious. "Bridget has recommended a therapist the club uses. I've got my first session next week. I'm hoping it'll make things easier to talk about. I want to manage my grief, I'm tired of running from it."

"I'm so proud of you." I wish I had more words to express that, but right now, seeing him so vulnerable and nervous, I can't think of anything that would do this feeling justice.

I lean up on my tiptoes, and we come together. We're grinning like idiots as we kiss. It's sloppy and messy but we don't care. All we focus on is each other.

"Do you think therapy is something we can do together? I mean, I understand if you want to go alone. But..." I trail off.

"You'd do that for me?" he asks hopefully.

"Of course. I can't begin to imagine how you felt all those weeks, watching me go out onto that pitch and then for your worst fear to happen. If the roles were reversed..." My heart aches and my eyes sting just thinking about it. I don't know who is comforting who anymore but what I do know is that we're united. "This is something we can work on together. You and me."

He nods his smile forming a tight line, emotion in his voice when he leans down and brushes his lips against mine.

"Natasha Borthwick, I think I was meant to fall in love with you."

"She knows what she's doing up there," I laugh, tilting my chin to the sky. "Because you're right, I don't think us falling in love is a coincidence at all. I think she made this happen."

CHAPTER TWENTY-TWO

Luke

Natasha is sleeping soundly in the bed next to me, with the quietest little snores and her chestnut hair a mess on the pillow; a result of the sensational morning sex we had about an hour ago.

It's been two weeks since we got back together. Two weeks of bliss, happiness and the best sex of my life with the woman I'm so head over heels in love with.

If you asked me when I agreed to plant-sit for my sister, if I saw myself falling in love with the gorgeous, sassy girl next door, I would have said yeah, because I'm pretty sure I fell in love with her the second I met her and loving her is the easiest thing I've ever done.

If you asked me if I thought she'd love me back, I would have laughed in your face.

She snuggles into my bare chest and lets out a small sigh of contentment when her hand settles onto my chest. Careful not to wake her, I pick up my phone and shoot a quick text to Bridget, checking the plan for later. She replies with a thumbs up, which I've come to realise isn't passive aggressive, she's just too busy to send full text messages.

No sooner have I put my phone back on the bedside table than Natasha's alarm goes off. It's a match day and we stayed at her flat last night so it wouldn't interfere with her sacred match day rituals. One day, when the time is right, I hope her rituals will continue at our own home together.

"Good morning," I say when her sleepy hazel eyes meet mine. "It's been a very good morning so far." She sits up and changes position so she's leaning down over me. She kisses me lazily until all the blood in my body, and hers too by the looks of things, heads south and it morphs into hungry desperate panting.

I hope we never lose this desire for one another.

I flip her over, settling between her legs as I pin her hands above her head, both of us still naked, my already hard dick pressing against her. She gasps as I kiss her, her back arching towards me and her hips wriggling, urging me to enter her.

"Again?" I ask, half of me hopeful and the other half knowing she's as insatiable as I am when we're naked together. She gives me a wicked smile as I snake a hand between us, still holding her arms above her head with my other. She's already wet. I moan at the feel of her warmth on my fingers as I push them into her, swallowing her gasps and moans as I coax her slowly towards a release. She grips my erection, stroking me back and forth as my hips involuntarily thrust into her closed fist.

"Tell me what you want, Nat," I say against her throat as I plant open-mouthed kisses on her pulse points, feeling it thrumming against my lips.

"I want you!" She pants and I rub my thumb against her clit. "Say the words, Nat," I groan, needing to hear her ask for it.

She cries out as I withdraw my fingers, tightening her grip on me and attempting to pull me closer. When she rubs the tip against her wet heat, I almost give in.

"What do you want, beautiful?"

"I want you inside me. I want to feel you fill me completely. Please, Luke, you're killing me here," she begs, and that's all it takes.

She screams my name as I push my hips forwards, filling her with one hard thrust.

"Luke, yes!" she moans as I drive into her with slow, deep thrusts just the way she likes it.

Dragging her fingers across my back and through my hair, she keeps me close to her, our bodies rubbing together as we move in unison. Kissing becomes impossible as we pick up the pace, both of us chasing a release. Instead, I bring a hand between us, toying with her and driving her closer to the edge.

I can barely hold on, especially when she makes those fucking incredible sounds of pleasure.

"Fuck! Yes! I'm coming!" she cries out as her body reacts to her climax. She trembles and writhes beneath me as I coax her through her orgasm, feeling her clench down around me until the last shiver leaves her body. Then my own hits as I push deep inside her with a feral growl, only stopping once I know I've filled her, giving her absolutely everything I have, exactly as she requested.

"Oh fuck." She sighs, then kisses me lazily. It's more than I can come up with. My brain is a heavily satisfied mush like my heart. Still inside her, I rest my forehead against hers, both of us breathing heavily as we come down together.

CHAPTER TWENTY-THREE

Natasha

When the team walk off the pitch later that day, narrowly avoiding relegation, the mood amongst us is intoxicating. It's the last game of the season and we scrape through by the skin of our teeth, but we all say the same thing as we huddle together on the pitch one last time: next season we don't want to find ourselves in the same position and we're prepared to do whatever it takes to make sure we don't.

As always, we stop to greet our fans and sign autographs on our way back to the tunnel. Something Luke said to me, weeks ago now, about the way these young girls look at me, stands out today because a young girl—she must be around six—is watching me carefully, her little sister bouncing up and down by her side.

"Hi, I'm Natasha." I hold my hand out to the young girls.

"I'm Amy and this is my little sister Ruby," she explains as they take their turns shaking my hand. "I'm going to be a goalie when I grow up." Her smile is so proud.

"Well, Amy, if you're going to be a goalie, you'll need

some gloves." I pull my gloves out from under my arm. "Here." I take a Sharpie from Brooke who is signing next to me and sign each glove before passing the pen back. "Now I want you to promise me when you're older and playing for Wearside, you'll remember me and bring me a pair of your gloves with your autograph, okay?"

I hand her the gloves and she nods, her eyes wide and excited. She throws her arms around me in a hug, and warmth spreads throughout my body as she thanks me repeatedly. I glance at her mam over her shoulder who mouths "thank you" with tears in her eyes. I sign Ruby's shirt and pose for photos with the sisters before making my way down the line of fans, taking selfies, listening to their stories and signing memorabilia until I get the nudge to get back to the dressing room.

As soon as I reach my locker, I'm pulling my phone out to text Luke to find he's already one step ahead of me.

I know it's hard for him to watch me play without remembering his mam, but the fact that he's here, supporting me every single match day means the world to me. Therapy is looking promising for both of us as we learn to navigate our relationship.

"Texting lover boy?" Brooke teases when she spots me grinning down at my phone like a lovesick teenager.

"Obviously," I say with a roll of my eyes.

"I honestly didn't peg you for the swoony type. Is this what happens when you have a man to worship the ground you walk on and give you mind-blowing orgasms on the regular?"

"Yup," I agree happily.

After I shower, blow dry my hair and apply a little bit of make-up, the lasses and I make our way up to the hospitality suite reserved for friends and family of the club.

As the team disperse throughout the ballroom to find their friends and family, I'm excited to see Luke sitting at one of the large round tables with Aaron, Bailey, Jordan and Bridget. Our other friends, Kieran, who plays in goal for the first team and Sam, former Wearside superstar, who now plays for Brighton, also sit chatting away to my boyfriend as if they're old friends.

I'm so eager to get to Luke that I almost don't notice the familiar older couple sitting at another table talking animatedly with Coach.

"Mam? Dad?" I ask as I approach them. They stand to greet me with matching smiles on their faces. When they hug me, I'm so stunned I can't even raise my arms to return their embrace. I just stand there, stiff as a board as they hug me. "You're here?"

"Oh, sweetheart," Mam says, her voice soft and affectionate as she looks over at my dad teary eyed. "We're sorry for the pressure we've put on you."

"You were fantastic out there," Dad says, uncharacteristically. "Unstoppable! You made us proud."

Emotion engulfs me and I dive into my dad's arms again, a sob escaping me as he says the words I've always wanted to hear. He rubs my back, comforting me, and I feel Mam's gentle touch too. Am I dreaming?

"I can't believe you're here."

"Your boyfriend gave us a good talking to, said we'd lose

you completely if we didn't get our act together," Dad says when I pull back. I look across the room to Luke in surprise, and he shrugs with a smile before coming to me and wrapping his arm tightly around my shoulder. "This chap seems like a good man. He looks out for you and isn't afraid to stand up for you, even to your grumpy old dad." Dad laughs and claps Luke fondly on the shoulder. I look between the men and wonder what twilight zone I have entered. I wish I'd been there for that conversation. I flash Luke a look that says, *you better tell me everything.*

"Can you excuse me for a second?" Luke asks, kissing my cheek softly before striding after Bridget, who appears from nowhere, tapping him on the shoulder.

"Better take our seats, your parents are safe here with me, you go on with the others," Coach says, rubbing my arm, and my parents take their seats next to her while I make my way to my seat with my friends.

"What's going on?" I ask suspiciously as Aaron pulls Brooke into his lap, making room for me to sit with them at the table next to my parents. As far as I know this is meant to be a quick *well done for not completely sucking* drinks reception. Not something secretive and fancy. After all, had we not won the game it would have been a *you're shit, here's some booze to numb the pain* party.

"No idea," Aaron replies, but the excited grin on his face says differently as he nods his head, indicating for me to look towards the stage.

Right on cue, a clinking of glass ensues, and the room

falls silent. "Well, everyone, I would like to raise a toast to our wonderful lasses," Bridget says. "We've learned a lot this season, we've experienced great losses and great wins and we live to fight another season in the WSL. We'll go into next season stronger than ever; the other teams won't know what's hit them. Cheers!" She raises her glass, and the room follows suit, echoes of cheers resounding throughout the crowd.

"We also have another announcement to make," Luke says when the applause fades out, taking Bridget's place at the mic. "For those that don't know me, I'm Luke Ramshaw and I've been hanging around the club for some time now researching a game I've been designing. Today, I can announce that I've been granted full funding to put this game on the market. So, without further ado, I present to you, WSL: The Legends."

The lights dim when Luke steps aside and a video begins to play on the projector screen. It's the first time I've seen the CGI footage from our day at the visual effects studio and I'm blown away at the quality. From our movements, Luke has been able to pull together a three-minute demonstration of the game, with graphics so lifelike, if I didn't know differently, I'd swear it was a video recording.

When the lights come up again, he steps forward to the mic and I'm on my feet with the rest of the room, clapping in sheer amazement and bursting with pride.

"I'd like to say thank you to Head Coach, Mel Libbey, and everyone else at the club for the time and effort you all put into helping me achieve this dream in honour of my late mother,

Lauren Ramshaw. And finally, I'd like to say a huge thank you to Natasha Borthwick, the absolute love of my life. None of this would have been possible without you."

The room erupts in more applause as Luke places the mic back in its stand and makes his way through the crowd. He crosses the floor quickly and when he reaches me, he sweeps me in his arms, dipping me backwards and kissing me as though there's no tomorrow. The crowd whistle and cheer and I can't help the grin that screams 'I'm the luckiest girl in the fucking world' from spreading over my face.

When he sets me upright again, he peppers more kisses to my lips until someone, probably Bridget, clears their throat loudly and we turn back to the group. I snuggle under Luke's arm, right where I belong.

Laughing, Brooke passes Luke and me a flute of champagne each and we all clink our glasses merrily in cheers. Together, we stand in out tightly knit circle, Jordan, Aaron, Brooke, Bailey, Kieran, Sam and Bridget.

"Congratulations, Luke and Natasha, I'm so glad you sorted your shit out and that Brooke didn't get a chance to chop off your balls," Bridget says, and everyone laughs.

"Never say never," Brooke says with a wink towards my boyfriend as we all take our seats.

"So," Bridget says casually, "I wonder what's in store for the rest of us."

EPILOGUE

Luke

Six months later

"Okay, here it is." Hannah hands me a small square jewellery box with a beaming grin splitting her face. Her knees bounce excitedly where she sits at the coffee table across from me. "The jeweller did a really great job of cleaning it up. It looks brand new."

I flip the box open with trembling hands. Mam's stunning teardrop engagement ring stares back at me. The large centre stone is emerald, the same as her and Natasha's birthstone, and the stones surrounding it are diamonds.

Just seeing the ring gives me butterflies and enough anxiety to send my heart rate through the roof.

"Do you think Natasha will like it?"

"Of course! She's going to love it." She grins. "When are you going to pop the question then? I'm dying over here. You've told me nothing!"

"Today." I look down at my watch. "In about an hour actually. And I didn't give you details because truthfully, I thought you'd have spilled by now."

When Hannah left for her trip to Australia, she and Natasha were friendly enough, but now, the two of them are as thick as thieves.

"That explains it." She shrugs as if her statement makes perfect sense.

"Explains what?"

"You're a nervous wreck. You have been all week. Natasha cornered me in the hallway the other day because you've had her so freaked out! I had to gaslight her into thinking it was all in her head, so please apologise from me when you propose."

She's right. I have been nervous. I know Nat loves me; she shows me every day in every single thing she does. But I still can't shake the fear that she might say no.

It is fast after all – we've been together less than a year. We're not even officially living together, despite not spending a single night apart, which is another thing I want to ask her today. I want her to move into my house. I want her to make it a home with me.

"Okay, I will." Letting out a huff of breath, I stand from my sister's couch, securing the ring box in the zip pocket of my running shorts, then double-and triple-check it's safe. "Right, I'm going." I walk towards the door, stopping when I grip the handle. "What if she says no?"

"Natasha loves you. She's going to say yes. Have fun and loosen up a bit." She smiles a big, excited grin as I finally swing open her front door and step into the hallway. "Try to enjoy the moment."

***

Natasha

"I'm telling you, something is going on!"

"I think you're overreacting," Bridget tells me calmly.

I can hear her typing, her nails clicking against her keyboard. She most likely has the phone propped between her shoulder and ear, her hair and makeup perfect as she handles some crisis with the grace of a swan.

Honestly, I wish I had her ability to always find calmness right now. I even tried to take a leaf out of Brooke's book and meditate. Much like the last time I tried that, it failed.

"Why else would he call me halfway through the workday and ask me to go for a run?!"

"I don't know, maybe he needs a break. You said yourself he's been stressed lately. Work is probably getting on top of him. Have you tried talking to him?"

"Yes, and every time I try, he does this thing where he…" I pause, wondering how much detail I should be giving away. "He distracts me."

Bridget lets out a loud laugh and the typing stops. "Okay, listen. It sounds to me like you both need to go on this run. Let it clear your head and I'm sure by the end of the day, you'll have your answers."

"What does that mean?" I jump on her statement as

114

though it's fact. What does she mean I'll have my answers? She knows something. "What do you know? You'd tell me if he'd had another wobble and was going to dump me, right?"

My greatest fear.

"I promise, I would tell you that. To be fair, I think it would be kind of obvious since Brooke threatened to castrate him and hang his balls from the Davy Lamp outside the stadium if he ever hurt you again."

"Oh yeah." I chuckle. "She really meant that, didn't she."

The door clicks open and Luke strides in using the key I gave him a few months ago. He leans down and kisses my cheek.

"Bridget, I've got to go, Luke just got here."

"Okay, have fun!" she sings before hanging up.

"Ready?" he asks, flashing me a nervous smile that doesn't quite light up his eyes as usual.

"Sure, let's go."

As soon as we start our run around the lake at Herrington Park, Luke is a different man.

The Luke I know and love. He's relaxed for the first time all week, and those jittery nerves? Gone.

Maybe Bridget was right, maybe I was overreacting.

We run the usual route, three steady laps of the lake and back up the winding path to Penshaw Monument. Having learned our lesson the first time we did this trail together, when we reach the bottom of the gravel staircase that leads up the hill, he takes my hand and we walk to the top together.

When we finally hit the top, instead of picking our usual spot between the centre pillars on the north side of the monument, we head to the back right corner which faces south.

"Luke?" A woman I don't recognise asks as we approach her.

"Yes. Hi." He reaches out to shake the woman's extended hand. Whoever she is, she mustn't know him well. "Thanks for meeting us here."

I nudge him, reminding him of my presence.

"Oh, sorry, this is my girlfriend, Natasha."

"I'm Anna, from the National Trust."

She holds her hand out to me too and I shake it, even more confused.

What is going on here?

Anna turns to the metal grate in the pillar, opening the hidden door with a large metal key.

In the summer the National Trust arrange tours where you can climb to the top of the stone monument, but they've been closed for weeks now the weather has turned. Although today is bright and sunny, there's a hint of autumn in the air evidenced by the red and brown leaves of the woods that surround Penshaw Hill.

"When you're ready, you can go up. I'll be right here if you need anything."

"Seriously?" I let out an excited breath as understanding washes over me. We're climbing to the top.

"I called in a favour with Bridget who called in a favour with someone else," Luke explains. "Every time we come up here you comment that it's on your bucket list. I wanted to make at least one of your dreams come true."

"My dreams come true every morning when I wake up next to you." I reach on my tiptoes and kiss him.

Is this why he's nervous? I know he's not great with heights but my balcony is higher than Penshaw Monument if you don't include the hill it stands on.

"You go first, the steps get steep at the top," he tells me.

It's cold inside the stone pillar with the sudden absence of daylight but I soon warm up again as I start to climb. The stairs are narrow, steep and never ending, and this exertion on top of our run has me sweating buckets.

"You know, I thought the best view would be at the top, but this view is amazing," Luke jokes from behind me as we reach the steepest part, my arse basically in his face.

"I'm glad you're enjoying it," I say breathless from the climb. "Give me a boost?"

With two palms on my bum and a little push from Luke, I emerge onto the open roof of Penshaw Monument.

"You did that for my benefit, didn't you?" He laughs, knowing I didn't really need the boost.

I flash him a mischievous smile in response.

"I love you," he says, reaching out to me.

Just three simple words have my anxiety easing. Was he really that nervous about coming up here?

I don't have time to think about it as his hands slide down my back to my bum where he pulls me closer with strong arms until I'm flush against his body.

My heart flutters as we kiss. Neither of us cares that we're sweaty from our run and climb, we're too lost in each other to even notice.

Reluctantly, he pulls away and smiles as if he knows a secret I don't. He turns me so I'm looking out across Sunderland, the real reason we're here. We can see even further than usual from up here and it's breathtaking. He settles into place behind me as we enjoy the peace and quiet. Content just standing together listening to the sounds of nature around us.

"Can you remember the first time we came here?" he asks me after a little while, the sun beginning to dip beneath the horizon.

"I nearly passed out right there." I laugh, pointing at the small wooden bench halfway up.

"Because you were trying your hardest to hate me and exerted yourself."

"I didn't stand a chance. I knew I wanted you the second I saw you even if I didn't want to admit it to myself."

It's true, one glance at his strong arms and beautiful collarbones had me weak at the knees.

"And look at us now." He chuckles. I smile and lean into him, revelling in the safety and security of being wrapped in his arms. He takes a steadying breath before continuing. "I didn't know it at the time but looking back now, I fell in love with you the moment I met you," he tells me.

"I don't know why…I was so awkwardly mean to you. You were half naked and, honestly, the hottest nerd I'd ever seen. I didn't know how to act."

He laughs and it illuminates everything inside of me. I'd do anything to hear that laugh for the rest of my life.

"It was your feistiness. The way you planted your hands on your hips and told me off had me hooked." He takes my hands in his. "I don't know how I got so lucky to have you fall in love with me, but I'm so grateful."

"Luke," I say, brushing my hand over his cheek, "I love you so much."

He steps out of my embrace, taking one of my hands in his and reaching into his pocket with the other.

"Natasha Borthwick."

"Oh my god," I whisper as he drops to one knee in front of me. Tears fill my eyes as I clasp both of my hands to the sides of my face.

"It would help if you could hear this." He laughs, and I move my hands from my ears.

"Sorry," I swipe at a rogue tear, "sorry, continue." I sniff, doing my best to compose myself.

It doesn't work so Luke carries on regardless.

"I can't imagine my life without you. I truly believe my mam sent you to me at a time when I needed you most. I was ready to give up on everything I'd ever worked for until I saw how strong and resilient you are, even if sometimes you don't believe it. I know it's fast, we've been together for less than a year, but I knew right away that you're always going to be my person." He takes my left hand in his, the pad of his thumb rubbing against my bare ring finger as he speaks. "I love you and I'll keep loving you every day for the rest of my life if you'll do me the honour of marrying me?"

"Yes!" I say on a sob, happy tears streaming down my face. "Oh, Luke! I can't wait to marry you!"

He slides the beautiful teardrop emerald ring onto my finger. It's a perfect fit.

"This was mam's ring. I think she'd be happy to know you're the one wearing it."

I'm crying harder when he stands and takes my face in his hands, using his thumbs to wipe away my tears before kissing me softly.

"You've made me the happiest man in the world, Nat. I can't wait to start the rest of our lives together, starting with taking you home, to our home."

I nod, letting out a hiccup and unable to tear my eyes away from the beautiful ring. I can't think of anything else I'd rather do right now.

THE END

Continue the series:

Playing For Her: https://mybook.to/B0BYD85WFH

Playing For Real: https://mybook.to/PlayingForReal

Coming Next

Playing For Real

Book 2 in the Wearside Story series.

Coming 25th April 2024 and available to pre-order now.

Aaron Milburn is one scandal away from losing out on the newly vacated captaincy at Wearside FC.

The captain of the women's team, Brooke Davison, is done with feeling like a side character in her own story.

When Aaron needs a little help with his ruined reputation, his long-time best friend agrees to be his fake girlfriend.

Although, the couple soon learn it's hard to fake it with someone you've secretly loved since childhood.

https://mybook.to/PlayingForReal

The Romance Retreat

Book 2 in the Romance Redefined series

Jackson McIntosh is desperate for an escape, so when an opportunity presents itself to attend what he believes is an exclusive romance writing retreat, he grabs it no questions asked and heads to the Lake District.

Taylor Harrison needs a miracle to save her family's B&B so when a nearby hotel double books a romance retreat, she steps in to save the day hoping it'll save her in return. Taylor is surprised when the man who jilted her at the altar twelve months ago arrives as a guest with his new girlfriend. Luckily, she has a sexy, brooding writer ready to step in as her fake boyfriend.

One romance retreat, two unlikely singletons with undeniable chemistry thrown in at the deep end and secrets that could ruin everything... What's the worst that can happen?

https://mybook.to/TheRomanceRetreat

Also by Ellie White

Love and London
8 Years ago.

Maggie's life was just as she had planned... Perfect. She had graduated Uni with Honours, had landed her dream job and was married to her childhood sweetheart. One thing that wasn't part of the plan was becoming a widow the night before her 22nd Birthday.

Present time.

Turning 30 has forced Maggie to start asking the difficult questions in life. Should she start using anti-ageing eye cream? How much money should she be paying into her private pension fund each month? Is she finally ready to start dating again?

When Maggie's Dad and his business partner Ray decide to retire early it's up to Maggie and Jake, Ray's arrogant and egotistical son, to take control.

Encouraged by her family and friends, Maggie embarks on an emotional journey of healing and self-discovery as she takes on new challenges, pushes herself from her comfort zone and finds herself on a string of terrible blind dates. All the while Jake tries his best to prove to Maggie that after years of antagonising her, he's not as obnoxious as he has had her believe.

https://mybook.to/B08T4WVT3D

Love in the Wings

Harriet Adams was a West End rising star until a lapse in judgement cost her her dream job, her boyfriend and so called friends.

She packs up her life and moves back to Sunderland where she gets a rare second chance at a career she thrives in. As she's about open a shiny new musical in front of a home audience, she vows that this time, nothing is going to get in her way. With everything riding on this, she'll play it safe, work hard and most importantly, stay away from theatre guys.

Cue Liam Wright, Assistant Stage Manager.

Liam is everything Harriet didn't know she needed in her life, but he also has a secret. One that could advance his own career if he cashes it in. The only catch? It would ruin any chance of happiness with Harriet if she finds out.

Harriet and Liam share a love like no other, but will that be enough to save their budding relationship when the time comes?

https://mybook.to/B0B2H95LJQ

A Romance For Christmas - A Novella

Zara McIntosh and Noah Williams fall in love at Christmas. The problem is, he's her older brother's best friend and no-one knows she's secretly divorced.

Christmas Day will test them, but will their relationship survive?

https://mybook.to/Aromanceforchristmas

A Wearside Story

A football romance series with a difference.

Playing For You

Ellie White

A prequel to the Wearside Story series.

Natasha Borthwick is Wearside FC's Number One, but after an embarrassing string of losses, she's not so sure she deserves that title anymore.

Luke Ramshaw is the hottest developer in the gaming industry but as his deadline to complete his funding application fast approaches, he still has no game demo to present.

The pair are thrown together by a meddling mutual connection in a last-ditch attempt to save both Natasha's team and Luke's career. The problem? They didn't exactly get off to a great start, but what happens when they get closer is a whole other ball game.

<u>Playing For Her</u>

Book 1 in the Wearside Story series

A tragic injury forces footballing legend Molly Davison into early retirement. Football is her life and now that she can't play anymore, she embarks on a new path as a coach for Wearside FC.

Captain of the team, Jordan Robinson, is preparing to hang up his boots at the end of the season and after being in the game his entire life, he's having an existential crisis. Not to mention the only woman he's ever had feelings for is back on Wearside, worse still, she's officially off limits.

Molly is Jordan's new coach, she's building a reputation for herself in the men's game and paving the way for women just like her. Staying away from the team captain should be a no brainer but when their chemistry sizzles on and off the pitch, it's easier said than done.

A romance that was once so easy has new challenges as the pair try to navigate their budding relationship through the world of men's professional football. Will their love risk the reputation Molly has worked so hard to build or can they finally have their happy ever after a second time around?

https://mybook.to/B0BYD85WFH

Acknowledgements

As always, this book wouldn't have been possible if it wasn't for my family and the support and patience they have when I'm on a deadline.

And a huge thank you to my wonderful editor Aimee, for helping me get the best out of these characters and their story!

Finally, thank you to my hype team! Chels, Louise, Melissa and Sophie. Thank you for all of your words of encouragement and your hilarious voice messages!

About the Author

Ellie White was born and raised in Sunderland and is a proud Mackem!

She lives in Houghton-Le-Spring with her husband and two young children. She supports Sunderland AFC and is a lover of chocolate, rom-coms, musicals and Formula One.

If you've enjoyed this book please leave a kind review on Amazon, Goodreads or Instagram, not forgetting to tag her! It doesn't have to be much, just a few words will do; it will make all the difference!

Follow her on Instagram @elliewhite_writes or search for her on Facebook, Twitter and Tik Tok to stay up to date with new releases!

Printed in Great Britain
by Amazon

42467207R00076